CAST OF CHARACTERS

FAMILY
SECRETS

In Emerald Cove, blood is thicker than water.

Holt Evans—The privileged playboy thinks the annual regatta is the most important thing in his life—but will his long-legged competition prove there's more important matters of the heart?

Marisol Villoria—Desperate to prove her racing skills, she's agreed to captain her own team in the regatta against her longtime rival. But has she taken on more than she bargained for?

General Bruno DeBruzkya—Is he truly the mastermind behind the attempts to steal Evans Yachts submarine plans for the U.S. Navy, or are there darker agents at work?

About the Author

LILIAN DARCY

has nearly fifty Harlequin Medical Romance books to her credit, as well as a growing list of Silhouette titles. Her books have appeared on the Waldenbooks Bestsellers list, and she received a *Romantic Times* Reviewer's Choice nomination in 2002. Lilian is happily married, with four children.

Lilian says, "When I was asked to write a book for the FAMILY SECRETS series, I was thrilled but unsure of what to expect. After weeks of suspense, a package arrived from Silhouette containing background information and a sketch of my story. It was like opening a Christmas gift from a secret admirer...and just what I wanted!

"I loved the glamorous backdrop of yacht racing, the sinister notes of sabotage and my passionate Spanish heroine, Marisol. Playboy, blond hero Holt meets his match in this dark beauty. Sparks fly and storms break overhead before these two can tame each other."

RACING
HEARTS

LILIAN
DARCY

Silhouette Books

Published by Silhouette Books
America's Publisher of Contemporary Romance

Special thanks and acknowledgment are given to Lilian Darcy for her contribution to the FAMILY SECRETS series.

SILHOUETTE BOOKS

ISBN 0-373-61383-0

RACING HEARTS

Copyright © 2003 by Harlequin Books S.A.

This edition published by arrangement with Harlequin Books S.A.

® and TM are trademarks of Harlequin Books S.A., used under license. Trademarks indicated with ® are registered in the United States Patent and Trademark Office, the Canadian Trade Marks Office and in other countries.

Visit us at www.silhouettefamilysecrets.com

Printed in U.S.A.

FAMILY SECRETS

Henry Bloomfield (d.) m. Violet Vaughn (d.)

Extraordinary Five

Jake Ingram m. Mariah Daley

Gretchen Wagner m. Kurt Miller

Marcus Evans m. Samantha Barnes

Faith Martin m. Luke Winston

Gideon Faulkner
m.
Brooke Carter

Connor Quinn
m.
Alyssa Fielding

Evans Family

Russell (Russ) Evans
m.
Lynn Van Allen

Charles Evans
m.
Sarah Alexander

Seth Evans
m.
Emma Carpenter

Drew Evans
m.
Alison Myers

Laura Evans
m.
Austin Brady

Honey Evans
m.
Maxwell Strong

Holt Evans
m.
Marisol Villoria

——— Birth Family
----- Adoptive Family
m. Married
d. Deceased

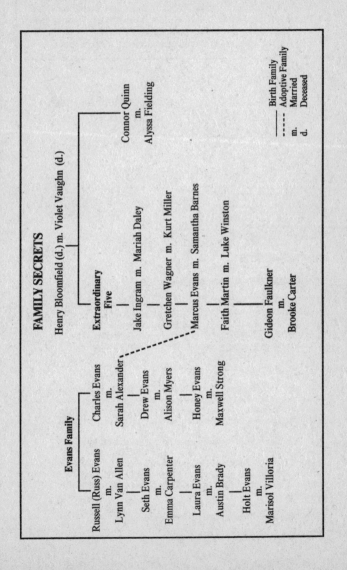

One

"Your father isn't here yet, Marisol."

"Oh, he's not?" Marisol answered in Spanish, the same language Renaldo Tejerizo had just used. She frowned. "I wonder where he is. He wasn't at home this morning, either."

She had flown in from Madrid just last night, and slept deeply, but jet lag had woken her early this September morning, at five-thirty. Thinking that her father was still asleep, she'd taken a long lap-swim in the heated swimming pool, splitting the swim down the middle with her daily weights routine. Oh, that beautiful, milky soft, blue-green Florida pool! She remembered it so well from when she'd lived here in her teens, but until this morning hadn't actually seen it in twelve years.

Not until after her shower did she discover that the house was empty, and there was no indication as to where her father was. The team meeting was scheduled for nine, here at the Clipper Bar, only now it appeared he wasn't here, either. It was strange.

"Come into the back room. We're ordering breakfast."

Renaldo turned without waiting for Marisol's reply. He obviously assumed she would follow him, and she did, although, as usual, she didn't much care for his abrupt style. He was a skilled yachtsman, however—a burly man of thirty, not tall but very strong, unmarried and devoted to the pastimes of a bachelor.

"She doesn't know why he's not here," he announced in Spanish to the nineteen men and one woman grouped around several large tables in the Clipper Bar's spacious private back room. Since some of the crew were local Americans and didn't speak the language, and all the European crew members spoke reasonable English, it wasn't the most considerate language choice.

Most of the group wore the Villoria team jacket, with its distinctive V of deep sea-green fabric, front and back, teamed with white sides and sleeves. The name *Villoria* was lettered boldly in white against the green V on the back.

"I'm not concerned about Fernando," Xavier Gonzalez said.

"Or Diego?" Renaldo asked, and Marisol realized that Diego Ruiz wasn't here either.

"We would have heard if there was a problem, wouldn't we?" Xavier asked. "I want breakfast!"

The words found an echo in the discreet growling of Marisol's empty stomach, which was still operating on Spanish time and clamored for lunch. Two hours of lap-swimming and weight-training didn't help.

Team manager Violetta Gonzalez, Xavier's wife, slid her chair sideways to make room. They greeted each other briefly, then Marisol sat down and picked up a menu. She ordered the biggest breakfast on it. Eggs and bacon and breakfast sausages. Home fries, whole wheat toast, pancakes and syrup. Pink grapefruit juice and strong coffee to wash it all down. Oh, and an order of biscuits and gravy on the side.

The order didn't stand out from the others in any way. All of the crew were eating big today. They'd probably been working around the boats this morning, or maybe they'd taken one of them out to drill their maneuvers or test some new piece of equipment.

Marisol's heart gave a little leap of anticipation as she remembered how good it felt to sail these Florida waters. The September day was bright and hot outside, and she could see a steady breeze whipping up harmless, lacy whitecaps on the sparkling water.

It was on a day much like this, twelve years ago, that she'd sneaked out of the house and entered an unimportant little Laser class solo yacht race without Papa's permission. She'd beaten Holt Evans by thirty-seven seconds to take first place.

The memory wasn't a good one. Papa had been furious and had packed her off home to Spain three days later. He'd taken a much harsher stance on her racing back then. Sixteen-year-old Holt had been even angrier....

"Here he is, at last," Renaldo said.

For a moment, Marisol thought he meant Holt himself. She knew he had to be here in Emerald Cove, and that their paths would cross soon. He would be part of the locally-based crew Evans Yachts had put together to race in next week's regatta.

At twenty-eight, he'd earned a worldwide reputation as a brilliant, tough and fearless yachtsman, bringing even more prestige and success to his family's already acclaimed boat design and construction company.

He'd earned quite a reputation as a babe magnet, as well.

"Twenty after nine," someone said. "And he doesn't look happy."

Marisol realized they were talking about her father. The Clipper Bar sat right on the waterfront, and the back room of the restaurant was built over the more informal oyster bar downstairs. It had windows overlooking both the marina and the street. They could all see Fernando Villoria. He strode toward the front entrance, his jacket open and whipping in the breeze, and his face etched with forbidding lines.

For a man of sixty-one, he was impressive, still as strong and straight and confident as ever. His thick, iron-gray hair was swept back from his high forehead, emphasizing the arrogant beak of his nose, and his arms were as thick and hard as pine logs.

He disappeared from view, and everyone waited. Seconds later, they heard his impatient footsteps and then saw him in the doorway.

"There's some bad news, everyone," he said at once. "I'm sorry, I didn't see any point in leaving a message, and anyway, I've hardly had time. I wanted to tell all of you in person. Diego had a heart attack last night and he's in the hospital in Miami. I've been with him all night and it's taken me more than an hour to get back."

The waitress put Marisol's breakfast in front of her at that moment. The woman had obviously overheard the news and looked wide-eyed and curious. Marisol's appetite fled at once, and she stood up without even feeling her body move. Diego…in the hospital…heart attack.

Her father's eyes met hers, and she saw that they were narrowed and watchful, and that his mouth had tightened with concern.

"Is he going to be—" she began. Her voice had gone husky and faint. She tried again. "How is he, Papa?"

"He's recovering from the surgery. They performed an emergency by-pass. Of course it's out of the question that he can lead the team, or even compete."

More steaming plates of breakfast appeared, to be set down in front of a silent crew. No one even looked at their food. Marisol slowly lowered herself back into her seat, aware that her father was still watching her. He wanted to know what she felt.

So did she.

She was stricken and shocked, obviously. Shaky. Tearful. More than that, however, she felt too numb to know.

"Diego is our captain. He was to skipper every race except the Laser-class solo." Renaldo stated facts that everyone already knew, but Marisol understood his blank shock.

Diego Ruiz was Papa's best friend, his right-hand man, and by far the most experienced sailor in the Villoria team. Only one person in the racing crew had sailed anywhere near as much as Diego, and that was Marisol herself—and then only because Papa had been bringing her onto his yachts, letting her roam around his boat-building yards and sending her out with his crews since she was six weeks old.

"Eat," her father ordered. "Everybody eat. Diego will be all right. The world hasn't stopped today. The regatta hasn't been cancelled. It most definitely hasn't

been cancelled! We don't want the Evans crew or anyone else to think this will give them an edge. Eat,
Marisol.''

Obediently, she picked up her fork, as did the others, and several mouthfuls disappeared from each plate
in silence.

"Who will take his place?" Renaldo finally asked.

Everyone turned to Fernando.

"That's the decision to be made, isn't it?" he said
slowly.

Marisol put down her fork again. The food tasted
like cardboard, in any case, filling her mouth with un-
welcome sensation and bulk. She had to struggle to
force it down. Papa had something on his mind; she
could tell. Something beyond the obvious concerns.

Everyone was still looking at him, their faces ex-
pectant. There was always a special atmosphere
amongst elite sailors, as the Villoria crew were. Accustomed to it, and yet a little apart from it for many
years, Marisol never knew quite how to describe it.

They possessed an odd combination of restlessness
and focus, and a perpetual hunger, not just for the
enormous meals that fueled their huge expenditure of
energy, but for the ocean, the boats, the race.

This morning, her father's news had added something even more unsettling to the mix, and she felt
claustrophobic, desperate to finish this meeting and
get outside.

"Diego himself—before he went into surgery—
suggested a replacement," Fernando said.

Mouths paused in their chewing. Eyebrows lifted.
Several people looked at Renaldo. He shifted in his
seat and blurted, "Well?"

"He thinks the role should go to Marisol."

Renaldo's fork clattered onto his plate. "You're joking!"

"No. Not at all. And neither was Diego. I told him— No, I won't tell you what I told him. Marisol, I'd like to hear what *you* have to say to the idea."

Papa wanted something from her, Marisol could tell. The only problem was, she didn't know what it might be. He had been setting up such hoops for her to jump through for as long as she could remember.

Tests.

Challenges.

Traps.

She knew that it came mostly from love and pride. Habit, too. Papa did the same to each of her four older brothers, on occasion. She didn't know how they felt about it. She had been a late, unlooked-for child, and wasn't close enough in age to her brothers to have earned their intimate confidences. But she got very tired of Papa's manipulative games.

Gritting her teeth to mask a sigh, she answered, "I know the Villoria boats inside out, since I've watched them being built and helped to test them in ocean conditions. I know Diego's plans and strategies for every race, and his observations on local winds and currents, because he's spent hours bouncing his ideas off me. I've competed with Villoria crews in European waters for the past six years, longer and more consistently than anyone else in the current team, although I haven't ever competed—" She stopped for a fraction of a second, then quickly added, "—elsewhere."

She'd almost said "here." This wasn't true. There

was that one small, insignificant race she'd won here at fifteen.

The race Holt Evans had taken so casually that she'd been able to power past him in the final five minutes. The race after which every other competitor had heard Holt publicly question her gender identity, with a sixteen-year-old's callow cruelty. The race that had made Papa so angry that he'd sent her home to her grandmother in Spain, to be turned into a proper female and to get this racing nonsense out of her head. Sailing as part of a family tradition was one thing; professional yacht racing was another, and he hadn't wanted it for his daughter back then.

She had no desire whatsoever to remind *anyone* about that race twelve years ago, so she said "else-where" instead of "here" and looked at her father, waiting for his response.

"That's not an answer, Marisol," he said.

She lifted her chin. "No? All right, then. Yes. I want to be the new leader of the Villoria team. I'll enjoy the challenge, and I believe—I *know*—I can do it."

Wrong answer.

This wasn't what her father had wanted.

She knew it the moment she saw the new shape of his mouth and the slight shuttering of his lids over his dark eyes. He hadn't wanted her to rise to the occasion. He'd wanted her to turn it down, to tell him that she appreciated and valued Diego's faith in her, but she knew she wasn't up to it.

Papa hadn't wanted to go against Diego's suggestion openly, for reasons she understood very well, but he'd wanted to get his own candidate in place, all the same.

Renaldo.

It had to be Renaldo.

Across the table, the man simmered. Staring down at his half-full plate, he tried to hide the fact, but no one was fooled. He'd wanted the leadership role, and Papa had wanted it for him.

"You have a lot of faith in yourself, Marisol," her father said. "You always have had."

Not in all areas of my life.

"But, Fernando—" Renaldo began. He earned only a dark frown.

"And Diego shares that faith," her father went on.

Diego is in love with me, Marisol thought.

"So we will regard the matter as settled," Fernando concluded. "Congratulations, my daughter. You are the new leader of the Villoria racing team."

Team manager Violetta Gonzalez set up a cheer and everyone joined in. Marisol's father waited for it to subside, the smile falling quickly from his face.

"We have a lot to talk about," he said. "There's the press conference at one, here at the marina. We'll announce our new captain then. We'll need more coffee, Violetta. Find the waitress, would you?"

The meeting finished after eleven. Marisol's neck and jaw ached. Three cups of coffee had made her jittery, and jet lag made her feel as if she was seeing the world through panes of slightly foggy glass.

As the group broke up, people talked, pushed back their chairs, looked at the weather outside and checked their agendas for the remainder of the day. Renaldo still looked angry and disappointed. She heard him mutter something in Spanish, while looking in her direction. He ended in English with the two words *rail meat*. A reference to non-sailors who went along for the ride in certain races, it wasn't an accurate description of her role and her capabilities, and it certainly wasn't a compliment.

Should she give Renaldo and Papa what they wanted, and announce that she'd changed her mind? Marisol wondered.

Stubbornness soon answered the question. She wouldn't give in to her father's games, nor to Renaldo's glowering hostility. Let Papa be open about what he wanted! She could respect that. More important, Diego's faith in her had touched her heart, as well. He believed she was up to this challenge, and she felt a tender need to prove him right.

"You'll visit Diego in the hospital, won't you?" her father asked at that moment. He came up to her and took her arm in his strong grip, speaking to her under cover of the buzz of talk that had risen in the room. "Take my car."

"Of course I will. Right after the press conference."

This brought a more satisfied look to his face. "He cares about you very much, Marisol."

"I know that."

"Don't make the mistake of taking it for granted just because he's been in your life for so long. Don't think you'll find someone better, because you won't. And don't keep him waiting much longer."

Well, she'd wanted openness from Papa. Now she was getting it.

"I—I have to make that judgment for myself, don't I?"

"You could simply take your father's advice. But I know you. You won't. Your head is no doubt full of some shallow, immature notion of romantic love, while poor Diego—"

"I can only feel what I feel, Papa," she told him, her jaw clenched tighter than ever. "I have to work out what that is, and whether it's enough."

"And meanwhile, I shall be sixty-two at my next birthday. A father only wants to live to see his children settled, but sometimes even that is denied—"

"Oh, give me a break! Where's the violin music in the background, Papa? You're as strong as an ox, and you know it!"

He had the grace to look ashamed, and they both laughed, diffusing some of the morning's tension.

"Don't miss the press conference," he said after he'd kissed her on each cheek.

"I won't." She straightened the collar of his team jacket as she spoke. "I just need some air. And some peace."

The rest of the team planned on going back to the hotel, or they had errands to run or work to do on the boats, while her father had a private meeting scheduled with Violetta. He sent his team manager in search of the waitress again, for yet another pot of coffee.

Marisol wasn't sorry to see everyone disperse. Slipping her sunglasses into place, she loped down the steps of the Clipper Bar and headed for the security checkpoint at the entrance to the section of the Emerald Cove marina where the racing boats were moored. Violetta had given her the required photo ID pass at the team meeting, and she received the security guard's nod and passed through with no problem.

Interest in the Emerald Cove Regatta seemed unusually high this year, putting the biggest events in the schedule almost on a par with more traditionally renowned races such as the Newport-to-Bermuda, or the British Fastnet, which Marisol had competed in last year. There were already crowds of people about. Tourists, reporters, yachting enthusiasts, racers from rival boats.

Sections of the large marina remained open, but there was no public access to the network of docks where the racing boats were moored in the water or suspended in cradles and slips. Larger teams such as those sponsored by high-profile corporations and those of the Evans and Villoria companies had their own security in place, also. The boats were alarmed, locked up, draped in concealing canvas and sometimes even guarded by a rostered crew member at night.

Marisol knew that such precautions were necessary. She'd heard a rumor that at least one of the Evans boats was expected to showcase something new. It wasn't unheard of in the yachting world for one team to try to steal another's innovations in equipment and race strategies, although actual sabotage was rare.

This morning, with the sun bright in the sky and the breeze cooling and fresh, such dirty dealings seemed out of place and not worth a thought. The synthetic ropes whipping against aluminum or carbon-fiber masts played a familiar music, and Marisol could see motor launches and sailing boats with furled sails leaving the docks and heading toward the other keys and the open water.

She would have loved to be amongst them, at the helm of *El Duende,* the fourteen-foot Laser-class craft in which she would be competing solo on Tuesday. With the press conference in less than two hours, however, there wasn't time. Instead, she wandered over the maze of wooden walkways, soaking up the sun and the atmosphere and the fresh scent of salt water, until she reached the single long dock where the Villoria boats were moored.

She was at the far end of the marina now, distanced from much of the noise and activity. She pressed a button on the key fob in her pocket and deactivated the electronic alarm of the biggest yacht, an eighty-foot maxi named *Skyrider,* which had been built here at the Villoria boatyard in Emerald Cove.

It was the exact twin of a boat she'd sailed countless times at home in Spain. Same hull design, same fittings, same sophisticated computer equipment, same extensive wardrobe of sails.

The tide had reached its lowest ebb, and the boat deck lay parallel with the level of the dock. With sure feet, she made a light leap across the gap between dock and deck, then clambered toward the bow, sat down and stretched her legs out in front of her on the warm white fiberglass, leaning back on her hands and lifting her face to the sun.

Her jacket fell open at the front, letting warmth strike her neck and chest above the white tank top she wore beneath. The heat's caress relaxed the tightness in her neck and temples and jaw, and it felt good to be alone. There wouldn't be very much solitude over the next ten days.

Would she be able to prove that Diego was right to

believe in her? she wondered. Had he known that Papa wanted Renaldo for the role? He'd stuck his neck out for her, if he had. He knew how arrogant Papa could be when he believed he was right. She had to make this work!

Too restless to accept the soothing radiance of the sun any longer, she scrambled to her feet in time to see Renaldo and Xavier coming toward the boat.

"Feel like playing monkeys this morning, Marisol?" Xavier said.

She looked up at the dark silhouette of the mast, which stretched skyward, clothed in its network of rigging. "What needs to be done up there?"

"Couple of things," Renaldo answered, taking her acquiescence for granted. "I'll get the equipment. Don't go away!"

Marisol waited while they fiddled around in the spartan cabin below deck. Leaning on the shiny metal railing that bordered the deck, she could see beyond the two adjoining shorter docks, as far as another longer one that stretched parallel to this.

Those were Evans yachts moored there. She recognized the team colors of turquoise and metallic gold, and the eye-catching Evans logo—the simply stylized gold silhouette of a sailing boat, set against a turquoise background, within a gold circle. The turquoise reflected the color of the water, and the gold flashed in the sun.

Something else caught the sun over on the Evans dock, as well—a man's head of sun-bleached hair. That wasn't Holt, was it? Watching him for another full minute, Marisol soon became certain that it was.

Twelve years had gone by since they'd last met, but

she'd seen photos of him in yachting magazines several times—clutching winners' trophies, mostly, with a smear of white zinc cream across his nose and a satisfied grin on his tanned face. He hadn't changed much.

At sixteen, he'd already been nearly six feet tall. Now he was even taller, and he'd filled out, as fit and strong as a young lion. He moved over the deck with a barely contained energy, and the gangliness he'd had twelve years ago had gone, replaced by a practiced athleticism and confidence.

Even from this distance, you could be in no doubt that this was a man who knew his world, and owned it. Marisol had had such a clumsy, painful crush on Holt twelve years ago. It had smoldered for months, impervious to his brash arrogance. She had no doubt he'd be an even more dangerous male to care for now.

Another man emerged from below deck on the Evans boat. His build was similar, but his hair was the color of sunlit syrup rather than straw. Holt's older brother, Seth? Very likely. Eight years older than Holt, he had already finished college by the time Marisol had started high school, but she'd seen him on several occasions.

Seth had been present, she remembered, on the day of that ill-fated race. He had been listening when Holt's best friend had asked him, "Doesn't it suck getting beaten by a girl?"

And he'd heard Holt drawl in reply, with every intention of being overheard by as many people as possible, including Marisol herself, "Oh, she's a *girl?* Really? Someone should tell *her* that, because it sure doesn't show!"

Seth had been watching when Holt's insolent six-teen-year-old gaze had swept up and down her bean-pole of a figure, had focused on the face sprinkled with freckles but bereft of makeup, the salt-chapped lips and the hair chopped off at shoulder level and scraped clumsily back into a wind-whipped ponytail. Seth would have heard Holt's bevy of pampered cheerleader-blond admirers giggle at his words, and he would have seen them staring and sneering at Marisol.

Yes, that was definitely Seth Evans, and the other man was Holt, and suddenly twelve years didn't seem like such a very long time.

Two

"Something happening over on *Skyrider?*" Seth Evans asked his younger brother.

"A couple of people about," Holt said. "I'm not sure if they're actually doing anything."

"Any rumors about whether they've got anything special on their boats this year?"

"Not that I've heard. Innovation is our department, isn't it? Villoria is more about building well-tried boats and using classic race strategies and doing all of it as perfectly as possible."

"It's brought them some impressive results."

"I wouldn't argue with that."

They both looked across at the other boat and Holt lifted his hand to wave at the figure on deck. He didn't know who it was. Female. Villoria's team manager was a woman, he remembered. Possibly it was her.

Whoever she was, she waved back, lifting her arm gracefully. The sleeve of her green-and-white Villoria team jacket slipped back, and a piece of jewelry on her wrist caught the sun. She had dark hair, worn long and looped back somehow, and she wore sunglasses. He could see little more detail than that.

"Fernando's daughter is racing with the team, I heard," Seth said.

"Apparently. She's been doing it for a while. We

haven't met up because she's stuck to the European races, inshore and some blue-water, but they've made some changes in the crew lineup over the past six months, and she's supposed to be here.''

"That represents a change of heart on her father's part, doesn't it?"

"Sure does," Holt agreed.

Twelve years ago, he remembered, she'd been forced to sneak into even a minor race without Fernando's permission. He'd been so angry, he'd sent her back to Spain within days. Now it appeared she'd talked him around, hammered his opposition.

Fernando Villoria was no pushover, and even though his only daughter was the apple of his eye, he'd never spoiled her. On the contrary, gossip on the racing circuit suggested he'd been harder on her than on his four boys.

Holt wondered what this said about the woman Marisol Villoria now was. He imagined she must have to be a pretty scary character—shrewish and graceless and as tough as old leather.

"Maybe that's her," Seth suggested.

"I doubt it." Unconsciously, Holt clenched his teeth as he spoke. Seth gave him a curious glance, but he pretended not to see.

He didn't have pleasant memories of Marisol. Twelve years ago they used to see each other all the time around the docks and in school. She'd had a crush on him, of course. He could have counted on the fingers of one hand the girls who hadn't. He'd been used to the fact, and he'd made use of it at times.

This didn't mean that he'd liked it. And he particularly hadn't liked it in relation to Marisol.

For a start, she wasn't the kind of girl most sixteen-year-old boys wanted to be seen with. She was awkward and shy and different, derided openly by the cheerleader crowd. Growing up in a household of men after her mother's death when she was ten, she knew nothing about being female. Instead, she gave the impression that she'd rather have been a boy.

And she was so emotional. She wore her heart not only on her sleeve, but throbbing. Holt might have considered having her as a friend, since they had sailing in common, except that every time he spoke to her, she would flush darkly as far as the roots of her hair, chew fiercely on her lip and seem incapable of making a coherent reply.

His friends teased him about her.

She laughed too loudly. She tried too hard. She actually thought she would impress him by beating him in that race!

After they had both crossed the finish line, she'd maneuvered her little craft toward his and shouted across the choppy water, "There, Holt! What do you think of that? I won!" Her whole body had looked electric with excitement.

"Yeah, did you notice I got knocked half-unconscious just before you overtook me?"

This was an exaggerated claim. The blow from his boom swinging across had barely raised a bump on the back of his head.

"Yes." She'd frowned, and looked concerned. Her brows were thick and black. "I saw that. Are you okay? I would have tried to help, only you sat up and kept going again. You weren't watching for your boom coming across when you tacked."

Holt hadn't been impressed that she'd turned his excuse into a criticism, although she was right. Already complacent about an imminent victory, he hadn't been watching. It was an elementary mistake. Sixteen-year-old boys didn't enjoy having their elementary mistakes pointed out by ugly-duckling fifteen-year-old girls who'd just beaten them in a race.

Holt had already been in a black mood when his friend Kurt had badgered him, back at the marina, about how it felt to get beaten by a girl. He couldn't remember anymore exactly what he'd said, but he knew he hadn't answered the question, and he hadn't been kind.

So, how did it feel?

It sucked, big time, to get beaten—not just by a girl, but by anybody. Racing was *important*. Holt hadn't realized it until that day. He'd taken it for granted that he would win without trying very hard. He had an Evans boat, and Evans know-how, and a natural talent that came from heaven knew where. He breathed it into his lungs from the salt wind, maybe. Or the Florida sun radiated it into his bones.

Of course he would win.

But that day he hadn't.

Clumsy, embarrassing Marisol Villoria had beaten him.

And if Marisol could beat him, other people could. And if people beat him too often, he wouldn't get to do this anymore. His father would start talking sternly about his future after college. "You have to get serious about a profession." Holt *was* serious! He wanted to race full-time. He already dreamed of the Whitbread and the Fastnet and the Sydney-to-Hobart.

Following the wake-up call Marisol had given him, he'd had sense enough, even at sixteen, to see that there was work to do. If he wanted to make yacht racing his profession, his life, then he had to be good at it. Not good at it half the time, through luck, or Evans backing, or natural talent, but good at it consistently, through effort and practice and strategy, through studying weather systems and wind patterns and ocean currents, through getting his level of fitness up to the max and keeping it there.

It wouldn't help his family if he lost. People would blame the boats. People would say he had coasted on the strength of his father's expertise, and that wouldn't reflect well on either of them. No one would want him on a crew.

He didn't say anything to anyone about this change of attitude. In fact, he did his best to hide it from his friends. Not cool, at sixteen, to appear too serious about life.

Twelve years later, it was a habit he'd kept. Very few people were permitted to see what was really important to him.

Twelve years later, he was one of the most successful and most renowned blue-water yachtsmen in the world, with a Whitbread, six Fastnets, two America's Cups and four Hobarts under his belt, sometimes in Evans boats and sometimes crewing for other teams—mostly those with top-level corporate sponsorship.

He had scored wins or high-place finishes in most of the big races he'd sailed, and he owed this success, more than he wanted to admit, to an embarrassing and ugly Spanish duckling called Marisol.

"...arriving Friday night. We'll put on a meal at the house for those who get here in time. They're coming in two different groups. Anyhow, that's where my thinking is right now."

Seth stopped, obviously waiting for Holt's reply.

"Uh, yeah, right," he said.

He hadn't heard a word.

The woman who probably wasn't Marisol Villoria had twisted her long hair into a tight knot high on her head and was climbing up to the top of the maxi yacht's mast. She had a tool pouch strapped around her waist. The black carbon-fiber mast reached to a dizzying height, but she showed no fear and moved with speed and grace.

"No, I want your opinion, Holt," Seth said.

"On what?"

"On whether to have them for dinner at the house," Seth repeated patiently.

"Sounds fine to me."

Holt concealed the fact that he'd only just realized Seth was talking about the flotilla of high-ranking naval officers and their aides who were due to show up next week. Camouflaged by the influx of visitors for the Emerald Cove Regatta, they would be shown the prototype of the radical new Evans Stingray submarine, now complete in almost every detail.

The Stingray project had picked up enormous momentum since Holt's adopted cousin Marcus's extraordinary brother Gideon Faulkner had come on board earlier in the year. Holt had been stunned to learn, some months ago, that by birth Marcus was one of a family of genetically engineered children with superhuman abilities.

Since this revelation, he'd heard the stories of all of Marcus's Extraordinary Five siblings, including the sixth child, who was long believed dead. Having been separated since childhood, each bore a different last name, and each had suffered through their own quest to trace and reconcile the past—a hellish quest, in some cases.

The Code Proteus project, once funded by a highly secretive scientific research wing of the CIA, had been abandoned long ago, but its legacy continued to play out, for evil as well as for good. A group of renegade agents had tried to recover the data on the long-ago genetic experiments and gain control of Marcus and his siblings, but they hadn't succeeded. Holt knew that much of what had happened to Marcus, Gideon and the others in recent months would never be made public.

Apart from Marcus, whom he had known as a cousin most of his life, Holt felt closest to Gideon. It was strange, when on the surface they couldn't have been more different. Jake Ingram, Gretchen Wagner, Faith Martin and Connor Quinn were only acquaintances to Holt as yet, but Gideon was becoming a friend, and his wife Brooke was a pretty incredible woman, as well.

With top level national security involved, however, Holt knew he wasn't going to be told any more about Code Proteus, Gideon's work on the submarine, or the visiting team from the Navy, than Seth and the others needed him to know. Being out of the loop made it hard to concentrate at times, such as now, when Seth attempted to fill him in. The boat on the Villoria dock captured his interest more easily.

The woman who almost certainly wasn't Marisol Villoria had reached the top of the mast. She slid a taut yet curvy behind into the flimsy sling of the boat-swain's chair already suspended there, reached into her tool pouch and got something out of it, then started. What? Unscrewing something, maybe? Holt couldn't see.

"Little brother," Seth said.

"Yes, Seth?" he replied politely.

"Focus."

"Sure."

"Kindergarten-level lecture in national security is-sues coming up, okay?"

"Okay, Seth."

"The sun doesn't rise and set according to your personal race calendar, by the way."

"I know that, Seth."

"Okay. So, as far as protocol goes, dinner at the house is appropriate, since the family and the business are so closely bound up together."

"Catering's not too bad at home, either," Holt added helpfully.

"Exactly. On the other hand, we could be in trouble if there's any truth to the intelligence we've received. We're told one member of what could be quite a size-able team of Rebelian spies may in fact be a serving U.S. naval officer who is part of the visiting group."

"The computers in our house are linked to the com-puters at the boatyard, and at company headquarters," Holt said, "although we have a pretty complicated series of codes to navigate before we can get into any of their programs these days. Do I get an A for this class, now?"

"Maybe." Seth's expression was still stern. He was only half-serious about it, but half was enough.

"Fill me in on Rebelia, Seth," Holt said. "It's been in the news a lot lately. The U.S. is not real impressed with its new leader, apparently. Bruno Bouzouki."

"Bouzouki, Holt! Good grief! That's a—"

"Kidding. Greek musical instrument, I know. I admit, I'm not sure how to pronounce the guy's actual name."

"Bruno *DeBruzkya*—" Seth enunciated the word with exaggerated care "—orchestrated the assassination of the Rebelian royal family in order to gain power, so the U.S. is not exactly a friend to his government. Since Rebelia is landlocked, he's using the neighboring country of Holzberg as a conduit to the sea, and trying to build his own navy."

"Trying to steal his own navy, you mean?"

"Exactly. He's a megalomaniac and he's having more success in his corner of the world than our government likes."

"And he wants the plans to our sub? How's he funded? Power-mongering and espionage on that level is expensive."

"Remember the illegal drain of funds from the World Bank last year?"

"He was behind that?"

"He was involved. And so were—" Seth stopped. "Look, you know the deal on this, Holt. There's a lot I haven't been told, and even what I do know, I can't tell you much about."

"Believe me, I'm not sorry! I've got my own agenda to think about, with the races this week." He glanced across to the other dock once more.

The woman who absolutely, positively, couldn't in a million years be Marisol Villoria seemed to be putting a replacement piece of equipment into position. A bracket of some kind? It was giving her trouble. The men on deck called suggestions up to her. She wrapped one arm around the mast and leaned out at a precarious angle so she could follow their gestures.

If Holt hadn't had a superb head for heights himself, even in gale-force winds and with a forty-foot swell, he would have felt ill just looking at what she was doing. He took a breath.

"Seth," he said, "the guy's not exactly going to excuse himself after coffee and pretend he wants to go off and play a game on the family computer."

"You think I'm being overcautious?"

"Over is better than under. On the other hand, having them in the house could make it easier to scope them out, get a handle on who might not be genuine."

"Okay, now you get an A. That's where I was leaning. I just wanted a second opinion. Have them at the house. Pull out all the stops. Make the guy feel safe, welcome, *trusted.*"

"Sheesh, she's going to fall! No. No, okay, she's holding on again. She can't be the team manager. I wonder if she's racing, or if she's part of the shore crew...."

Seth's hands clamped to each side of Holt's head and turned it away from the direction of the Villoria dock. "There are other teams, Holt, you realize, and there are other boats. There's *Omega* and *Lavazzi* and *British Blue.* There's even a little outfit from a company called Evans, who hold important U.S. naval contracts, as well as building and restoring world-class racing and pleasure craft.''

Holt looked his older brother in the eye and sighed. ''You're going to make a great Dad, do you know that?'' he said softly.

''What?'' Seth blinked. ''Why?''

''You just are. Great combination of patience and firmness and humor. Emma should hang on to you.''

''I think she's planning to.'' Seth tried not to smile, but failed. The contented grin of a recently and happily married man with a pregnant wife spread across his face.

''Dinner for the naval officers at the house.'' Holt clapped him supportively on the shoulder. ''Good strategy.''

''Thanks.''

At that moment, Holt's cell phone tinkled out a tune more appropriate to a passing ice-cream truck, and he answered it.

''Holt, where are you?'' It was Tori, his date for tonight.

''On the *Unicorn*.''

''The what?''

''I'm on a boat, Tor. You know I'm always on a boat.''

''Hm, I should know that, by this time, shouldn't I? Well, I'm at the salon and I need to know what you think about my hair.''

''Your hair is beautiful. I've always thought so.''

''Don't be an idiot, Holt. I mean for tonight. Up or down? Formal or simple? Or there's this style I'm looking at right now, in a magazine, where—''

"Tori, seriously, your hair will look beautiful no matter…"

She'd finished the job. The non-Marisol woman on the Villoria maxi had finished her task at the top of the mast. She shimmied out of the boatswain's chair and swarmed back down toward deck level. She had the sleeves of her jacket pushed up to the elbows, and that bracelet, or whatever it was, caught the sun once more.

Her very feminine hips rocked from side to side as she made her descent. Right when she reached the deck, her hair fell out of its knot and tumbled down her back like a dark chocolate waterfall. Holt had an enormous fondness for chocolate.

He took a tight breath and managed to finish his assurance to Tori. "…whatever the heck you do to it."

"Thanks, Holt," she drawled.

"You're welcome. I have to go, okay?"

"Of course you do!"

"Work to do on the boat, and then there's a press conference at one, but I'm already going to be late."

"Tonight?"

"Late for the press conference."

"I'll see you tonight, right? Let's get it straight."

"I'll pick you up," he promised.

"Thanks, lover."

Tori's voice cut out, replaced by the brrr of the dial tone. Holt barely noticed. The woman who wasn't Marisol had just crammed her flowing hair up into a green Villoria baseball cap. She unfastened her tool pouch and said something to the two men now working at the bow. Seconds later, she disappeared into the cabin below deck.

Three

Marisol left the press conference early, after doing what was expected of her.

A lot of interest surged in her direction from reporters and rival teams when they heard of Diego's illness and her new role. Her father announced how proud he was, how much confidence he had in his daughter, how hard she had worked and how much she deserved this.

She fielded some tough questions from the *Daily Envoy*'s Bridget Vaughn and a couple of other reporters, deferred on several technical issues to Renaldo, and then she left, with the keys to Papa's car in her pocket.

Although the Evans team was represented at the conference by several crew members, Holt Evans was not one of them. She heard someone from the team say that he'd be here, but he was running late.

As her father had said this morning, the drive to the hospital in Miami took over an hour. Leaving the interstate, Marisol could see the hospital buildings, just as Papa had said she would.

A helicopter flew low overhead, its rotor blades beating the air. She saw it land on the roof of the main hospital building, against a backdrop of city haze, and realized it must be a medical emergency chopper, bringing a critically ill or injured patient for surgery and treatment.

Locating an empty space in the visitors parking lot, she heard an ambulance siren whooping louder and louder as it approached, and as she walked in the direction of the main entrance and lobby, she passed the emergency entrance and saw a patient being raced in on a gurney.

These dramatic sights and sounds, with their life-or-death significance, focused her mind on the reality of Diego Ruiz's illness in a way that the distractions around the Emerald Cove marina had not allowed.

Diego might have died today.

He hadn't died. He was going to be fine. Papa had called the hospital right before the press conference, and Diego was recovering well. His surgeons were confident.

But it might not have worked out that way. How would she have felt if...

Marisol didn't know, but wished with all her heart that she did.

It took her several minutes to navigate her way to the intensive care unit. Directed to Diego's private room, she found him lying very still, with eyes closed. She paused in the doorway. Was he asleep?

He looked older than his forty-nine years, much older than when she'd last seen him two weeks ago at the marina in Marbella, the day before his flight to the U.S. His face was pale and slack and locks of hair lay flat and damp against his head.

A lump thickened in her throat, and she came close to tears.

This shouldn't be happening. Diego was *young*. His

hair was still more black than gray. He was fit and hardy and capable. He had a twenty-year-old son from his short, failed marriage many years ago, and he maintained such a good relationship with Carlos that the two of them were more like brothers or friends than like father and son.

Marisol approached the bed slowly. She didn't want to waken him. But he must have heard her, or felt her presence. His eyes opened as if with a great effort. She knew he'd only been out of surgery for twelve hours. He was hooked up to half a dozen monitors and tubes, and the pale-blue-patterned hospital gown seemed to mock his masculinity. A nurse had told her he'd only just had his breathing tube removed.

"Diego," she said.

He slid his hand from beneath the sheet and held it out. She took it, and felt the reassuring firmness of his grip.

"I'm glad you came, Marisol." His voice croaked.

"Of course I came!"

I'm so fond of him. I care so much for him, she thought.

Should there be more? Or was Papa right? Was this as much as she needed to feel? Was this what a woman should feel for her future husband? Marisol wanted a clap of thunder, something dramatic, like that helicopter landing on the hospital roof, bringing life-and-death certainty.

She leaned across and brushed her lips against Diego's cheek. He smelled of illness and antiseptic. There was a chair beside the bed, and she pulled it forward a little, then sat down, taking his hand in hers once more.

"How are you feeling?" she asked.

"Better, now that you're here. Better than I felt at four o'clock this morning. Pretty tired."

"Rest. Don't try to talk."

"You mustn't stay long. Too much to do. The captain's role... I told your father that the best person—"

"Yes, shush, stop tiring yourself. I know what you told Papa, and yes, I'm the team captain, now. Just for a month or so. Just until you're fit again."

He smiled.

She wanted to kiss him again. On the cheek, as before. Very lightly.

More than that?

No, she didn't hunger for it. She never had.

But maybe that was her fault, not his. Maybe with just the right romantic backdrop of music and wine and moonlight and laughter, if Diego seduced her, something new would blossom inside her and she would know that she loved him the way he wanted her to.

The way Papa wanted her to. Physically, romantically, with a full heart.

"Don't stay," Diego said. "Beat the traffic. But first, I want to tell you, at tomorrow's practice, make sure that Xavier—"

She couldn't stop him. He insisted on going through half an encyclopedia of instructions about the boats and the crew, making himself breathless. She realized it was better to let him say it all than to tire him further with arguments, and she even took notes. His nurse appeared and warned her, "You mustn't tire him like this."

"Tell *him* that," she answered.

Diego nodded. "Yes, it's my fault. I'm tiring you, too, when you have so much ahead of you. Go, Marisol."

Tears streamed down her cheeks as she drove back to Emerald Cove. She didn't know why she was crying. Because she cared too much for Diego? Or because she didn't care enough?

Either way, she had to pull over before she reached the house, dry her eyes and wait until the redness subsided, because if Papa saw her like this he would have questions, and she didn't have answers right now.

"Holt, is it true that *Unicorn* has a radical new keel design in place?"

Holt recognized a journalist from one of America's premier boating magazines. He smiled at the man. "Do you really think I'm going to answer that, Mr. Barber?"

"Do you really think I'm going to believe that *Unicorn* has her hull and keel covered in a big blue plastic skirt out of feminine modesty, Mr. Evans?"

Everyone laughed.

"There are lots of reasons to cover a hull," Holt said. "Protection against damage. Ongoing work. Maybe we've refinished her, and she's like a bride. Doesn't want anyone to see what she's wearing until the big day."

More laughter.

There was a sense that the main business of the press conference was done with. The Emerald Cove Regatta publicist brought it formally to a close, and people broke up into smaller groups. Several journalists approached racers for private interviews. Crews huddled together, discussing what they'd just heard.

Holt found that he kept looking for the familiar green-and-white Villoria team jacket. He saw several, but if Marisol was racing with the team, she wasn't here right now.

Finally, he asked a fellow racer from *British Blue*, the top maxi from the United Kingdom.

"She left early," the man said. "She took some heat for a while, with the questions people threw at her."

"Why is that?"

"You haven't heard? She's just been made captain and she's going to skipper several of the races, unusual for a woman in a mixed crew, even in this day and age. Ruiz is in the hospital. Emergency heart bypass, Villoria said. Gives the rest of us an edge, I should think."

"Yeah?" Holt answered. "I've heard she's pretty good. She was the last time I raced her."

"And when was that?"

"A while ago." Twelve years, in fact. "I expect she's even better now."

He wasn't sure why he felt the need to stand up for Marisol, nor why he was so curious to see her again. He'd been filled with a powerless fury against her for months after their race. Teenage boys detested anyone who made them feel uncomfortable, anyone who drew attention to their own inadequacies, even by accident.

He wasn't a teenager anymore. He would hit thirty in thirteen months.

Maybe that was why he wanted to see her. He wanted to prove to her, and to himself, how much he'd changed.

Papa had warned Marisol that the party at the Evans mansion tonight would be huge. The state governor was planning to attend, as well as a clutch of celebrities from other fields of endeavor. Actresses, baseball players, pop singers.

There would be some more anonymous faces as well, but many of them would be even more important than the people whom everybody recognized. Corporate lawyers and successful businessmen didn't get their photographs in glossy magazines all that often, but they held a lot of power and influence in their hands.

And it was to be formal. Tuxedos and floor-length gowns, uniformed waiters, live music, platoons of catering staff.

Over the phone two weeks ago, Papa had told Marisol, ''Go shopping in those boutiques your friend the sheikh's daughter loves so much. Buy a dress, shoes, whatever you need. Don't even look at the price.''

Well, she'd ignored this last advice. She'd looked. She'd bought the dress and the shoes anyway, and still went dizzy when she thought about how much she'd paid. Studying her reflection in the dressing-room mirror of her suite at her father's house, she knew she'd never looked better.

The simply cut off-the-shoulder dress was chili-red, and the smooth knit, silk-sheened fabric hugged her figure with loving emphasis from breasts to hips, then flared out with the grace and movement of a flamenco skirt.

Papa's housekeeper had helped with her hair and had revealed an unexpected—and welcome—talent for creating an elegant pile of twists and tendrils on top of her head. Frankly, hair salons still numbered among Marisol's least favorite places in the whole world. Maybe this was why she'd stubbornly let her hair grow until it reached her waist.

Yolanda had done her makeup as well, scolding her throughout. "Sit still! Lift your chin!" Marisol was well accustomed to being scolded over such matters. Her beloved grandmother in Spain never let up.

"I must make sure someone takes a picture, so I can send it to *Abuelita*," she murmured. Then she laughed aloud. *A* picture? There would be photographers in attendance, blinding every guest with their flashbulbs at regular intervals all night!

Abuelita, I wish you were here!

She owed her grandmother so much....

It had taken Isabella Joaquin six years to turn a rebellious and self-doubting fifteen-year-old girl into a well-rounded young woman. *Abuelita* had made mistakes during the first year.

The perm, for example. The short-lived secretarial course. The ballet lessons. Marisol had responded unenthusiastically to all of this. She *wanted* to please her beloved grandmother, but she just couldn't. Not with that program.

Then one day *Abuelita* had looked at her, really *looked* at her, after she'd come in from a day on the water. Sunburned nose, salt-chapped lips, hair as crazy and tangled as the wild thyme bushes that grew on the rocky Andalusian hills, smiling with happiness and not even aware that she was doing so.

"Just look at you! You look so alive, and so content!" *Abuelita* had whispered, half to herself. "How can I do what Fernando wants me to do? You will *never* be tamed. You could never be cured of being who you are."

So they negotiated.

Things changed.

Marisol promised to brush her hair with a hundred strokes morning and night and to submit to a monthly conditioning treatment at Marbella's most expensive salon, if she was permitted to keep it long and straight. No more messing with blow-dryers and curling wands.

Abuelita substituted gourmet cooking lessons for the unwanted keyboard and computing classes, and the passionate dynamism of flamenco for the detested and tightly controlled poses of classical dance. A well-bred modern Spanish girl from a wealthy family needed to take classes to round off her education, but at least the new classes appealed to Marisol's sensual and passionate spirit.

Abuelita helped Marisol to find out who she was, and to live in harmony with that person. It wasn't easy. It took time. And there were compromises. For at least four years, during her father's frequent visits, Marisol understood that he was still disappointed in her. They argued constantly about the issue of racing, and he was implacable.

The answer was no.

She couldn't defy him. He had Diego Ruiz on his side. Diego, who would calmly and cheerfully take her out with a crew to test new sails or new hull designs for hours on end, day after day, and just as calmly

and cheerfully refuse every time she argued that Papa
would never know if, just this once, in the twilight
regatta next Saturday, she was allowed to take her
familiar place on the boat.

Eventually, she gave up. She was just as passionate
as ever about sailing, and took to the water as much
as she could, but she poured more of her soul into
other pastimes as well. Adulthood loomed, and the
reality that she had to do something with her life. She
had no desire to laze her days away with shopping
and tanning and partying, before and after an inevi-
table marriage, the way many daughters of Marbella's
well-heeled elite preferred to do.

With her skill in French and Spanish cuisine, she
thought about starting a restaurant. She discovered a
love for traditional Spanish fabrics and designs, and
wondered if she could possibly base herself in Florida
and open a boutique there, featuring designers and
goods from Spain. She considered working on the
business side of her father's still-growing company,
possibly as its publicist, and wondered if Papa would
encourage this ambition or crush it.

She realized that if any of these scenarios was to
be workable, she had to present herself well, and that
all *Abuelita*'s teaching about posture and grooming
and manners and conversation was in fact necessary
and useful and important.

When her father and her two Florida-based brothers
came home to Marbella for her twenty-first birthday,
she was on tenterhooks, ready to talk to Papa about
her plans. She would need his financial backing in the
early stages to launch a business of her own.

Biding her time, waiting for the right moment, she

saw him several times locked in private conversation with Diego, and then suddenly, out of the blue, the night before her birthday, Papa said to her, "So, this racing business. This obsession with boats. Have you grown out of it, yet?"

"No, of course I haven't! It's in my blood. *Your* blood, Papa! The genes I inherited from you!"

"Diego says you have enormous ability."

"Does he?" She had flushed with pleasure.

"We've talked about it. He thinks you should race with the Villoria crew, and it seems to me that you are ready."

"*Ready?* I've been ready for—"

"No, you haven't. Now you are."

"Oh, Papa!"

Flinging her arms around his neck and covering his sun-hardened face with kisses, she had hardly registered his next words. "I must tell your grandmother how pleased I am with all that she's done."

More than six years had passed since that day, but Marisol hadn't forgotten her elation, nor had she forgotten her grandmother's lessons.

As satisfied with her appearance as a level-headed woman could ever be, she slipped into her heeled chili-red shoes, but abandoned the beaded red clutch that lay on the bed. She hated carrying a purse, preferring to keep both hands free.

Her father called from the corridor, "Ready, Marisol?"

"Yes, here I am."

He didn't say anything about her appearance, but she had learned over the past few years to recognize the satisfaction in his eyes. It made up, just a little, for his doubts over her new role with the team.

Everything looked just right, Holt thought as he came downstairs. A family pride that he still didn't feel fully comfortable with, and still only rarely let show, swelled inside him. Beside the sprawling and luxurious house, sheltered by Spanish-style adobe walls from the salty breath of the sea, the lush and extensive gardens were magically lit, as was the patio surrounding the pool, and the terraces leading down to the Evans family's private marina.

The ocean was almost a part of the place. The day's fresh breeze had dropped and the waves lapped gently against the boats. If conditions were like this next week for the races, the competitors would go nowhere. Tonight, however, it didn't matter. The balmy stillness was perfect.

Guests had begun to arrive, stepping out of limos or handing the keys of their vehicles to the parking valets who waited discreetly on the steps that ran up to the big iron gates. In the spacious linked reception rooms that overlooked the water, long tables draped in white linen held stacks of gleaming glasses and piles of china. The china's custom-made design in turquoise and gold suggested the colors of the Evans logo.

In the kitchen, Holt heard a crash, followed by a string of cursing. He smiled. Nothing in this life ever went perfectly to plan. Poking his head around the door to check on the situation, he was told, "Everything's in hand, Mr. Evans."

"Smells incredible," he answered, then slipped out a side door to go pick up Tori.

Four

Marisol saw Holt two or three minutes before he caught sight of her. Nerves coiled in her stomach and her skin felt hot. It was so stupid! Why should she feel that she had anything to prove to this arrogant specimen after so long?

He was wearing a tux and a blonde. Or maybe the blonde was wearing him. Either way, they accessorized each other beautifully, both of them such perfect advertisements for the Florida lifestyle that they could have been air-brushed and computer-generated, not real people at all.

She wasn't usually this catty.

Did the unkindness of schoolyard taunts still hurt so much, then, after all these years? And when she and Holt spoke to each other, as they would inevitably have to, would Marisol feel fifteen again?

She didn't want to!

She wished *Abuelita* was here. But her grandmother was over eighty now and didn't care to travel so far.

If she *were* here, what would she say?

Marisol found herself smiling. Did she really need *Abuelita* standing beside her and whispering in her ear? Hadn't she heard it all before, a thousand times?

"Stand up straight. Fill your lungs. Smile. Even when you're scared. Even when you don't know what

to say. The only people who can't make good conversation are those who don't listen. Smile, listen and
the right words will come.''

And that was when Holt Evans caught sight of
her—when she was standing there, listening to *Abuelita's* voice in her mind, when she'd straightened her
back, breathed deeply and was about to smile.

The Villoria team manager was standing on the far
side of the room. I'll go talk to Violetta, Marisol
thought. If I move now, he won't have a chance to
reach me.

But it was too late for that strategy. She'd hesitated
a fraction of a second too long. Holt had seen her, and
was coming toward her. She couldn't pretend that she
hadn't seen him. His date had detached herself from
his arm to go greet someone else. Marisol shifted her
champagne from one hand to the other and waited.
Holt smiled at her, and frowned at the same time. He'd
reached her now.

"I think we waved to each other this morning," he
said. "That *was* you, wasn't it? I wasn't sure at the
time. In the top of *Skyrider*'s rigging?"

She nodded, not yet able to speak. For a moment,
time seemed to hold its breath. This wasn't how she'd
expected to feel when she came face-to-face with Holt
Evans for the first time in twelve years.

"This is amazing. Marisol…" The Spanish name
was a whisper of sound across Holt's lips.

"Holt," she said, and her face flickered into a
smile. "It's—it's good to see you."

She looked stunning, Holt thought at once. And yet
she hadn't totally changed. Across the room, he'd
been in no doubt as to who she was. It was as if all

the things that had made her ugly and gawky at fifteen, all the things the clique of type-A girls at school had derided her for, had turned around, fought back and won.

She wasn't skinny and gangly anymore; she was as supple and straight as a young willow. Her black hair, once like a witch's broom, now gleamed on the top of her head, shot through with chestnut highlights that reflected the warm glow of the room. Her dark brows, once so fierce and forbidding, still gave strength to her face but now they arched high above her creamy lids, shaped by a professional's hand.

She'd lost that ever-present frown, and her smile was gorgeous. Her freckles, which used to look like a spattering of mud on a little boy's face, were now a sprinkling of nutmeg and fairy dust.

She used to dress as if she'd chosen her clothes in the dark. Now she was wearing a living flame. Holt hardly noticed the cut of the dress, nor its detail. All he saw was the color, and the way it fit as if it was part of her, making him deeply aware of the lush, athletic body beneath.

The roar of party sounds faded in his ears, and he was oblivious to the other guests. He cleared his throat. "I hear you're racing now. Heading up your Dad's team for this series. Congratulations."

"And to you." Her smile was soft and natural. "Your talent has done so much for the profile of your family's business, Holt. I heard you won Newport-to-Bermuda on handicap this summer, and your maxi took line honors in Hobart two years ago."

"I didn't do it alone. We had a great team. Some of them are here. I should introduce you...."

He looked around vaguely, but couldn't see anyone from the team. He found at once that he was pleased about that, and realized he wanted to keep her to himself for a while. I can't believe this is the woman I disliked so much, for so long, he thought.

Tori was talking to an actor he faintly recognized from some recent movie. Mom and Dad and Seth worked the room. The roar of conversation was like the wind building to a storm at sea, while in the larger room beyond this one, live music played and people bobbed and gyrated in pairs. Cameras flashed at frequent intervals. Waiters kept coming from the kitchen with filled trays. No one looked bored or left out. The party was a success, and at the moment Holt's input wasn't required.

"Would you like to dance?" he asked. He wasn't remotely ready yet to let this moment go and to move on.

"That would be very nice." She had a light accent. Maybe she'd always had it, only she'd never said enough to him in their teens for him to notice it. Now it made him want to watch her mouth and the way it moved every time she spoke.

Her lips weren't poutlike and collagen enhanced, as were those of most of the women he dated. Their shape was sensitive, and very slightly flawed. The dent at the top was deep and a tiny bit crooked. He wanted to press his fingertip into it, as if his touch could brush it straight. His fingertip, or maybe even his mouth.

He put his hand in the small of her back for a moment as they made their way into the next room, but he didn't leave it there. Could it be that he didn't have the confidence? That he was nervous about her reaction? When had he ever been nervous with a woman?

Feeling his hand come and go, she turned and smiled at him, and he caught the tiny flash of uncertainty in her eyes also. She felt the same. Both of them were finding this…intense. More so than he would have imagined possible.

They reached the dance floor and he had a decent excuse to take her in his arms. That felt much better. The band was playing cover versions of light pop classics, and the current number counted as a slow dance. Laura and Austin, Holt's new brother-in-law, were definitely taking advantage of the mood. They danced so close together, they looked as though they were permanently joined.

Holt didn't hold Marisol quite as closely, but after a few short minutes, he wanted to. Her body was warm and strong, and her hair looked like black silk, shot with dark gold. He wanted to rest his cheek against it and find out how she smelled. There was a fragrance of orange blossom teasing his nostrils. Was that her scent?

He opened his mouth to ask her about it, planning to craft some easy line about the magical scents of Spain. They'd both been strangely silent since they began to dance. But his breath felt too high and full in his lungs, and he knew it would be an effort to get the words out.

For some reason, he didn't want to give her the kind of smooth, flattering line that normally came so easily to his lips. And then, way too soon, the band changed tempo and everyone broke apart.

Slow dancing, he quickly discovered, wasn't the

only kind of dancing that could light a fire inside a red-blooded man. The way Marisol moved, when she wasn't reined in by his own basic notion of dance steps, had him mesmerized. He locked his legs into a kind of step-shuffle, step-shuffle holding pattern and tried not to let on how much pleasure he took in watching her.

Hips making hypnotic figure eights. Waist going curvy and tight, curvy and tight, like a sail in the wrong wind. Breasts neat, high and round, and just full enough to bounce a little. Shoulders, carved like a Greek statue, came warmly to life.

Eventually, inevitably, she caught him at it. Her dark eyes widened, she stopped dancing and then she laughed, self-conscious. She touched her hair, lifting her chin with the movement, so that he could see the graceful lines of her neck.

Feeling as self-conscious as she was, he said the first thing that came into his head. "What's your training routine? You're fit."

Sheesh, what kind of a score should he award himself for a line like that? Not delivered with his usual easy flair, but at least it didn't sound as if his tongue was hanging out.

"I swim every day, and I lift weights," she answered.

"Sailors aren't supposed to swim too well," he drawled. "They're not supposed ever to need to."

She laughed again. Her laugh had changed, too, in twelve years. It was velvety and delicious now, warmed from within, as if by a wonderful secret.

"I don't care about that," she said. "If I was superstitious, how could I sail at all? Women on boats are traditionally supposed to bring bad luck." She added on a drawl that held just the slightest edge, "Along with bananas, some people say."

"Guess you've had time to knock that one on the head."

"Bananas? Yes, I've brought bananas onto a boat with no noticeable ill effects."

"I was talking about female sailors."

"Not just me, though," she argued. "Women have sailed solo around the world. There have been all-female crews contesting the Whitbread...how many times now, do you know?"

"At least three, I think. There was an all-female crew the year I did it. They beat us on the transatlantic leg. Tough, considering women physically just aren't as strong."

"Which is why I swim and weight-train. To get the endurance and lifting strength as much as I can."

"The weight-training doesn't show. I mean—" Holt swore under his breath. "It shows in—"

How about you try that again, bozo, he coached himself, with another muttered curse for good luck.

"I mean you look great, Marisol," he said. "That's all. You look incredible."

Some kind of alien life form had invaded his body. An alien from a planet where flirting hadn't been invented. He'd been smoother than this with girls at sixteen.

Crueler, too, occasionally.

Maybe this was why he felt so oddly unsure of himself tonight. He remembered too clearly the way he'd once treated her. Beneath the well-bred manners, beneath the glow, and although he was one of her hosts, Marisol probably detested him.

A familiar stubbornness set his jaw, and he felt a rush that had to be adrenaline—the same adrenaline he always felt before the start of a race. If she did have feelings left over from their awkward dealings with each other twelve years ago—if they both did— it was unfinished business. He was going to do something about it. He wasn't going to let it slide.

You couldn't win every race. Holt had accepted that years ago. Masts broke. Winds failed. Crews didn't pull together the way they needed to. But never yet had he been forced to accept that you couldn't win every woman. Not always to take to bed. He wasn't like that, despite his reputation.

But he'd never failed to win *something* from a woman, when he put his mind to it. Her respect. Her liking and trust. The secret understanding that she *wanted* him to take her to bed, even if she wasn't available and it was never going to happen.

And he was going to win something from Marisol, too, only he was left with the disorienting and unfamiliar realization that he didn't know what he wanted that "something" to be.

"Dancing isn't your area?" Marisol prompted Holt, after they'd gyrated aimlessly opposite each other for another song or two.

He looked as if his mind was elsewhere. Far away. Beyond the horizon. His blue eyes had narrowed—it was like the sun going behind a cloud—and she was convinced he'd lost interest.

Lost interest in what? What had he wanted from her in the first place? Too bound up in her own confused feelings, she had no idea. For a few minutes she would almost have sworn she sensed an answering chemistry coming from him, complementing his instant and horribly familiar effect on her own pulse points and nerve endings.

Now she wasn't nearly so sure. It was far more plausible that he'd simply been trying to size her up. He'd even talked about sailing and female racers. Like the sporting press, the big-league sponsors of the maxi boats, and the other crews, he wanted to know how much of a threat the Villoria team posed now that they had a woman in a key role.

She didn't know whether to be grateful or angry at the fact that he'd done his research on the dance floor, instead of simply shoving a microphone in her face and throwing questions at her.

Less confrontational, maybe, the way he'd handled it, but even harder to trust.

"Dancing isn't my area?" Holt echoed her question, pulling his focus back into place with difficulty. "No, I guess it's not."

"Then we should stop."

Marisol's chin lifted, and her eyes glittered—black, warm, a little skeptical. What did she think? That he wasn't enjoying this anymore? Maybe she was right. The powerful and seductive pleasure he'd felt at first had been swamped by other concerns. For the first time in his life, he was in the company of a woman who wasn't just post-race recreation.

She was a competitor.

She'd always been a competitor.

One time, she'd won.

And he didn't know how to deal with it.

The band took a break, and the drift of people
through the adjoining room and out onto the large
patio announced the arrival of supper.

"Hungry?" Holt asked Marisol.

"Yes, actually. I could eat a horse."

He gave a shout of laughter and it startled her. She
shot him a puzzled glance. Still grinning, he explained, "You don't know how long it's been since
I've heard a woman say that!"

"I'm sorry, I— Sailing is pretty physical, and—"

"Lord, don't apologize, Marisol! I didn't mean to
make you feel—" Just as she had, he seemed to be
finding it difficult to finish his sentences. "Of course
you have to eat. Around four thousand calories a day,
if you're doing it right. You race. I shouldn't have—
Here, let's grab some plates."

She nodded, took one and moved to the tables. He
hung back a little and watched her. Chef Manuel Zal-
divar had surpassed himself tonight. The huge buffet
of hot and cold dishes was redolent with the exotic
aromas of Florida's vibrant cuisine, a fiery tropical
mix of Latin America, Cuba and the Caribbean. Suc-
culent seafood, spicy salsas, Nicaraguan *pastelitos,*
salt cod fritters, Haitian chicken fricassee… It went
on and on.

Marisol piled her plate, closed her eyes and inhaled,
as earnest as a wine taster judging a new vintage. She
picked up a tiny yucca fritter with the tips of her fingers, dipped it in a puddle of spicy red sauce on the
side of her dish and popped it neatly into her mouth.
Her face showed bliss.

"Holt, lover… I'm so sorry!"

Holt dragged his gaze with difficulty from the almost painfully erotic sight of Marisol Villoria sampling her food. It was Tori who'd addressed him. In one hand she balanced a plate with a tiny portion of plain salad on it. The other hand came to rest, with a possessive, apologetic caress on his sleeve.

"Tori," he growled.

"I've been totally locked in conversation with Matt. I didn't mean to abandon you. He's directing now, and he's scouting locations right here in the Keys. I've promised to take him around tomorrow. I mean, we're not *exclusive*, you and I, right? And you'll be on a boat for, like, the next millennium, so—"

"It's fine, Tori."

"I even said— Well, the script calls for a night scene, apparently, and I said—"

"You can say it, Tor. You're ditching me, right?"

"Not forever." She winced.

It probably *was* forever. He didn't care.

"It's okay," he told her.

"Thanks, lover. I'm going to take him to scout the night location as soon as I've eaten." She gestured carelessly at her pitiful salad. "I mean, it's my career. You understand that."

"Just the way you understand mine."

Her eyes widened a little, but he knew she hadn't caught the irony. Maybe it wasn't fair of him to feel that she should. After all, he was used to it. Hadn't met a woman yet who truly understood the racing thing. Hadn't had a relationship yet that could survive it.

The Whitbread was a race around the world. Including training time, equipment preparation and testing, the Whitbread he'd sailed had taken up more than a year of his life. The woman he'd been dating when he set out from Southampton in mid-1997 had met him over seven thousand miles later in South Africa so they could spend some time together during the layover between the first two legs of the race.

Two weeks later, in the teeth of a rising storm pushing straight out of Antarctica, she'd faxed him on the boat, telling him it was over. She couldn't hack the separations, the hours he put in, the fear she felt on his behalf, and all for what? A dumb boat and the chance of a dumb trophy?

How could he answer that attitude? How could he explain what sailing meant to him?

He'd had a brief affair with a woman he'd met on the layover in Sydney, and she'd been interested enough to fly over to Auckland to spend some time with him during the layover there. But the Evans crew had had mechanical trouble with the boat and publicity commitments to their co-sponsors. Hannah had spent most of her time hanging around her hotel room waiting for him to find time for her. After those few snatched days they hadn't seen each other again.

All his relationships were like this. Destroyed by racing just as surely as a spinnaker sail got shredded in a high wind.

Tori ate her salad in two bites, abandoned her plate to a passing waiter, kissed Holt full and quick on the mouth and hurried back to her rising Hollywood star. Holt wasn't sorry to see her go. There were plenty of other people he could talk to. Plenty of other people he *should* talk to.

For some reason, Marisol was still the only one who drew him.

Attuned to the sound of her voice, he could hear it over the sea of supper-bound guests who now separated the two of them. She spoke in Spanish, talking to someone from the Villoria crew and to an older man. One of her brothers, Holt realized. It was Juan, the eldest of Fernando Villoria's four sons, who had to be around thirteen or fourteen years older than Marisol. He was based in Marbella, but Holt had met him a couple of times during Juan's visits to Florida.

Filling his plate quickly, Holt eased his way through the knots of people and slotted himself into the threesome of Marisol, her brother and her fellow crew member. None of them looked particularly happy to see him, but he didn't let that bother him.

"Can I get you a drink, Marisol?" he asked. "Or seconds?" He looked at her now empty plate and raised his eyebrows deliberately. "Thirds, maybe?"

She laughed. "No, not thirds. I do have limits."

Their eyes met, shutting Juan and the other man out of their private joke.

The adrenaline was back.

I want this, Holt realized. I want to be able to do this with her.

To shut out other people, even in the midst of a crowd. To make her laugh. To make her look at him with those huge, dark eyes and know exactly what she was thinking and feeling.

"It's getting hot in here," he said. "Can I take you outside and show you my mom's garden? She's very proud of it, and I think you'll find it reminds you of home."

"I'd like that."

He could hardly drag his eyes from her lips as she

spoke. They looked redder than before, and fuller, as if the heat of the chili dipping sauce had darkened them and made them a tiny bit swollen.

"Let me find the bathroom first," she added. "And a cool drink."

So, yes, she *did* feel the heat. Just the heat of the chili? Or the heat they'd generated in the air between them?

"Do you two guys know each other?" Juan asked Holt, as soon as Marisol had gone.

Holt looked at the man beside Juan and gave a perfunctory smile. "No, not really. Possibly from a distance, if we've raced."

"Holt, meet Renaldo Tejerizo. Renaldo, this is Holt Evans. Renaldo is a brilliant helmsman, Holt. I can guarantee he's going to give you some trouble."

"I'm looking forward to it," Holt said. "Racing isn't fun if the competition's too one-sided."

The brazen, deliberate arrogance of the statement had both men laughing. There was an edge to it, however. Beneath their pretended amusement, Juan and Renaldo didn't like the suggestion of Holt's superiority, even in fun. Marisol cloaked her own competitive spirit in softer colors.

The three men spoke for a few minutes more—about the weather forecast for the coming week, about the strength of the *British Blue* team. Then Juan said something in Spanish to Renaldo, and the latter nodded and slipped away through the crowd.

"Don't underestimate my sister, Holt," Juan said as soon as the other man had gone.

"No danger of that."

"And don't assume she's vulnerable in the way I've

heard most other women are vulnerable to your particular brand of charm.''

''No?'' Immediately, Holt didn't like or trust where this was going.

''Marisol is spoken for. However it may appear tonight, her heart is elsewhere, and so are her thoughts. They're in the hospital in Miami, where Diego Ruiz is recovering from his heart surgery earlier today. For this reason, my sister *is* vulnerable at the moment, as she would never normally be to a man like you. And if you attempt to take advantage of the fact, you'll regret it.''

''Juan, don't!''

With their gazes locked on each other's faces, neither Holt nor Juan had noticed Marisol's approach.

Juan's expression became bland and benign at once. ''Don't what, little sister?''

''Whatever you're warning him about—I'll pretend I can't guess!—it's not necessary. He's a competitor. We have plenty to talk about. I'm not going to give away any Villoria secrets. I can take care of myself.''

Juan shrugged. ''If you say so. You do have the option of being grateful for my interest and my care, Marisol.''

''You are so much like Papa, do you know that?''

''Again, you could be grateful for that. Papa loves you.''

Marisol turned away without answering her brother and ordered in a husky tone, ''Holt, show me your mother's garden.'' To her brother, over her shoulder, she added, ''Juan, let me know when you and Papa are ready to leave.''

She took Holt's arm and almost dragged him

through the press of guests. A young journalist tried to greet her, but she didn't even see him. Her strength of will was impressive, communicated directly through the way her body moved, the way her swinging hips bumped against Holt's thigh, the way her dress slipped a little from one shoulder as she pulled him forward.

"Wait," he said.

She stopped and turned, her expression still fierce and determined, her black eyes electric and her lips parted slightly.

"Is it true, what Juan said?" Holt demanded bluntly. "Are you involved with Diego Ruiz? Is tonight just a performance for you? An obligation, while you'd rather be at his bedside?"

She threw up her hands. "Is that all anyone wants to know about me? How I feel about Diego? I care about him very much. Tonight is not a performance, but yes, I wish he wasn't alone. But Diego himself is the last person in the world who'd want me to put my commitment to the team in second place. His faith and confidence mean so much to me. If another man could ever compete..." She shook her head. "I don't know if it's possible."

Hiding the abrupt flattening of his mood, Holt said lightly, "I'm sorry no one will leave you in peace on the issue. Maybe things would settle down if your engagement was formally announced."

She frowned. "Yes, I'm quite sure that's true."

"Good luck to both of you."

"I— Yes. Thank you."

"Do you still want to see the garden?"

"Yes. I'd like some air, and maybe if you're with

me, I won't look like an obvious target for more questions.''

"I'm glad to be of help," Holt murmured, disturbed by how much he craved the power to change the clouded expression in her eyes.

Five

In the middle of the following morning, two men strolled casually toward the jutting point of land that marked the western end of Emerald Cove, locked in conversation. The men were dressed casually, like hundreds of others in Emerald Cove today. They had medium-brown hair, cut into conservative, unremarkable styles, and they were neither conspicuously old nor conspicuously young.

"The wind has picked up," said the younger of the two.

"Yes," replied the other. "The boats are flying."

Dozens of boats moved on the water, and they watched the spectacle for a moment in silence. It was a magnificent sight. The sky was a cloudless blue, and the sun on the water dazzled and danced. Even the humidity had dropped a little today.

Brightly colored spinnaker sails ballooned in front of the yachts, catching the wind and making the gleaming hulls seem to skim the water. The racing crews were practicing, while pleasure boats zigzagged among them, their occupants working on their tans or enjoying their proximity to the elite yachtsmen.

"We should hope this atmosphere keeps up all week," the older man added. "From our perspective, the more activity this regatta generates, the better. It'll distract the Evans family, and we'll be able to lift the information we need on the Stingray sub and get it smuggled out of here.''

"You've approached our contact in the Evans boat-yard for another diversion?''

"I'm not using him this time unless I have to.'' The man scowled and gave a wheezy, absentminded cough as the wind hurled a flurry of dust in their direction.

"No?''

"He failed us before. The timing of the explosion was completely wrong, useless to us. How good is a diversion that happens so far from most of the people it is supposed to divert that they don't even know about it until several days afterward?''

"You're right. I have little patience with incompetence.'' The younger man, with the slight Rebelian accent, concealed the fact that he wasn't convinced the charge of incompetence should be laid at the Evans employee's door.

"The problem is, we needed Walker's weakness to give us leverage. However, weakness and incompetence too often go hand in hand, as they did in his case.''

"You have another candidate in mind, I presume?''

"Yes, or we'll have to make do with Walker after all. Time is running out.''

"We could always threaten him with more serious consequences if he fails us again.''

"I will, if it comes to that. But this new candidate should be a better bet. He's well placed to move around the marina at will, and he's trusted by those who count. He's experienced in mechanical and technical matters, and knows what he's doing around boats. Most importantly, he's disaffected.''

"With whom?"

"With the crew he's a part of. Villoria. That's the weakness we need to exploit. He's just lost out to the boss's daughter for the role of team captain, and it was a job he wanted badly.''

An observer could almost have seen the wheels turning in the younger man's mind, only there were no observers at the moment.

"You're right," he said. "It shouldn't be too hard to convince him that if he can blow the Evans boat— literally—out of the race and win for Villoria—''

"While making sure that the responsibility for the sabotage falls onto Fernando Villoria or one of his sons, of course.''

"—he'll be able to walk into a top position on another boat.''

"Not to mention the revenge angle. Mediterraneans are a hot-blooded, vengeful people. We Rebelians have cooler heads.''

"You're only half Rebelian, sir," the younger man dared to joke. "And wasn't your mother born in Delmonico, before the border changed?''

"I'm Rebelian. That is the part that counts, despite the uniform I wear most of the time." There was an edge to the voice.

"Of course. I didn't mean—"

"I'll use the invitation to dinner on Friday at the Evans house and our tour of the boatyard the next day to reconnoiter the security systems and the location of the plans. You've organized the hidden camera equipment?"

"That's right. We'll make a trial run with it today."

"And I'll find the right opportunity to approach Tejerizo within the next few days. I'm confident we'll get a result this time."

Beyond the wide mouth of the cove, the wind strengthened. Marisol felt it as *Skyrider* tacked back and forth, drilling the routine until every crucial, speed-stealing second of wasted time was trimmed from it.

With jet lag still skewing her body clock, she'd left the party rather early last night, before eleven. A part of her had wanted to stay. The dangerous part. The weak part. The part that couldn't stop thinking about Holt Evans, full of all the old, breathless, giddying sensations that had swamped her so disastrously in his presence as a teenager.

She hadn't let that part of her win, however. She'd used the issue of her involvement with Diego as a deliberate shield. More than ever, she and Holt were competitors, and she understood his charm and his charisma in a way she hadn't understood it at fifteen. He could play those games with anybody. With the right words, the right touch, the right looks, he could create that *estremecimiento,* that quiver of awareness, in almost any woman he chose.

Marisol felt it, and responded to it—*hugely,* if she was honest—but she didn't trust it or want it. She was stronger than she had been at fifteen. And she was wiser. After just ten minutes of walking with Holt through his mother's garden—ten minutes in which she had been very careful not to touch him, nor to stray toward personal subjects in their conversation—

she had asked him to take her inside and help find her
father.

"I'm tired. We have a full schedule tomorrow. I'm
ready to go home."

He hadn't tried to persuade her to change her mind.

She'd slept well, had fitted in the shorter swim and
weights program she went through on sailing days,
eaten breakfast and arrived at the marina at eight.
They had *Skyrider* out with its full crew of twenty-
two by eight-thirty, just as the wind began to pick up.

Most of the boats were out a little later than they
were. *Unicorn*, Marisol had noticed, seemed to be
having trouble with a new piece of equipment. She
saw Holt, but not close enough to speak to. Now, out
on the water, his boat still skimmed the waves at a
distance, changing sails for the fifth or sixth time.

Renaldo wanted to change sails, too. They were still
experimenting with exactly which ones they'd carry
with them during Saturday's race from Emerald Cove
to the Bahamian port of Nassau. "We've got a perfect
wind," the helmsman said. "Why this spinnaker? Go
up a size and we'll break twenty-two knots. More."

"And we'll shred the sail," she answered him.
"The wind's good, but feel how it's clocking around.
We can't handle that much power from the wrong
angle."

"We'd better try to," Renaldo growled, "or we'll
have a full set of pristine sails when the race is done
next Saturday, and we'll be in last place."

They glared at each other.

Who's watching? Who's listening to this? Marisol
wondered. Which of the crew are close enough to ob-

serve every detail of the way Renaldo is questioning my decisions, and my approach?

It was a lonely feeling. Who could she talk to? Papa would use any confession of doubt to further his own ends. So would Holt. And Diego must not be stressed by complaints and negative news. Journalists, competitors, other members of the crew? Lord, there was no one!

"Fine," she said to Renaldo. "You're right. This is a practice. Let's go to the edge of safety and see what happens."

The wind shifted quarter at that moment, gusting into her face.

"Tacking!" Xavier called out, and the "coffee-grinder" winches ticked and whirred frantically in the hands of the crew, crowded on deck.

"We're changing sails," she announced, and directed the crew to pull out the biggest spinnaker.

The huge green-and-white sail crackled as the crew worked. Marisol joined them. The old spinnaker came down and the new one ballooned aloft. At once, they could all feel the wind's new power seizing hold of the boat. Ropes, rigging and sails creaked and groaned.

Well out from land now, the water was much darker, showing its depth. With nothing to impede its flow, the wind drove across the waves in opposition to the powerful current of the Gulf Stream. As Marisol had noted, however, the wind was fickle.

The boat's speed hit an impressive twenty-four knots and they drilled through another maneuver. Jose, who was timing each movement, announced that they'd shaved a further two seconds off their previous best, and everyone cheered.

Seconds later, they hit a rogue wave and a rogue jet of wind, and the spinnaker blew out just as Marisol had predicted, ripping clean across with a violent sound. Flapping in all directions, it tore again and threatened to foul the equipment high on the mast.

"Down, down, down!" yelled Renaldo. "Get it in! Don't lose it! It could do damage."

They got the sail in safely, but Bjarne, a young Danish man and the most junior member of the crew, split open his hand in the process and dripped great splashes of blood all over the deck as he gyrated in pain.

"Get below," Renaldo rasped at him in English. "Get out the kit and get it fixed." Turning to Marisol, he said, "Twenty-five knots, did you see that?"

"Yes, and how fast are we going now?" she retorted.

Three or four knots at best, with their mainsail luffing like a loose piece of tissue paper and no spinnaker in place. Marisol could see *Unicorn* approaching rapidly on the opposite tack. The gap between the two boats would soon close to about twenty yards, maybe less, and *Unicorn* would pass in front of *Skyrider* off the port bow.

"How fast we are going now is not the point," Renaldo answered. "It was an exercise. We had to test the limits of the boat and of the sail."

"I knew their limits already."

"You couldn't have. Not so precisely. We have to push the envelope. If you don't understand that, you'll never win."

Because you're a woman, and women don't take the right risks.

Renaldo didn't say it, but Marisol knew quite well it was what he meant.

Turning away from him, she called out, "Let's get that first spinnaker back up."

She felt the distinct rock of *Unicorn*'s wake against *Skyrider*'s hull as the other boat powered past at impressive speed, with Holt Evans at the wheel. He made no sign that he'd even recognized the Villoria boat.

Marisol was wrong.

Holt had seen and recognized *Skyrider*.

He saw the spinnaker blow out, saw the boat lose speed, saw the frantic actions of the crew and sensed the tension on board, even at a distance. Certain members of Marisol's crew weren't planning to make her new role easy for her.

Holt had no issues with that attitude. If Marisol couldn't handle it, couldn't resolve it, couldn't earn her crew's respect, then she was the wrong person for the job. In the demanding world of yacht racing, this was simply a fact. You had to trust your crew, and they had to trust you. Lives depended on it sometimes, as well as millions of dollars' worth of equipment.

Right now *Skyrider* wasn't in any trouble, Holt noted. It looked as if someone had gotten slightly hurt, but the situation was in hand. He made sure of that. It was written into the rules of yacht racing that competitors must help a rival boat in serious trouble.

At the same time, he kept a close eye on what his own boat was doing, and at the moment when *Unicorn* passed in front of *Skyrider*'s bow, he was fully occupied in taking the rising swell of each wave at the right angle. As they surfed down the backs of successive waves, he noted with satisfaction that he was bringing the boat's speed up higher every time.

"I saw your sail get shredded," Holt said to Marisol that night at her father's house.

The party to welcome Marisol home to Florida was Fernando's idea, and at seven thirty the crowd had already grown dense and loud.

"Yes, it was the high point of our practice," Marisol answered him lightly. She handed him a drink and their fingers touched. The contact unsettled her more than it should have done.

Holt was careless about his hands. They were callused and hard. A sailor's hands. A man's hands. She didn't want to think about how many other women would have found their roughness and their strength attractive.

"It was bad luck," Holt said, still talking about the blown-out sail.

"In racing, there's always that." She didn't mention the conflict with Renaldo that had culminated in the spinnaker's violent explosion. Dissent within a crew wasn't a subject to share with your major competitor. Instead, she continued, "From what I saw, you had a good day once you finally got out. Whatever you had under wraps until this morning is obviously working."

The noise of music and conversation built higher, and they had to stand close to hear each other. Holt looked relaxed and comfortable in sand-colored pants and an open-necked knit shirt. He must have showered just minutes before arriving. Against his tanned neck, just behind his ears, his hair was still damp and he smelled as clean as Andalusian mountain air after spring rain.

"It's an experimental finish developed by my cousin Gideon," he said. "We applied it just to one side of the boat so we'd have an accurate comparison of performance between the two finishes in the same conditions."

"In theory, then, you should have gone faster on one tack than on the other."

"In theory, and in practice. The experiment worked."

"Are you supposed to be telling me this? Isn't it highly confidential?"

"That we'll have a technical edge over you next Saturday? I don't see why. The finish performed up to expectations, and we'll apply it to the starboard side of the boat in time for *Unicorn*'s big race. Villoria boats will probably be using it a couple of seasons from now."

"Villoria boats don't depend on the latest gimmicks."

"No good crew depends on them. They're a tool, an ingredient in the mix. I enjoy the challenge of getting the mix right."

Their eyes met, blue clashing with black, and suddenly there was a second meaning to Holt's words. Erotic. Suggestive. Had he intended it? Marisol didn't think so.

Incredibly, he looked a little startled by the moment, and by the way their gazes had locked together. As startled as she was. As startled as she had been

last night. She was far too aware of him. Fifteen again,
not twenty-seven. It made her breathless and tense.

"Here comes my father," she murmured, relieved
at the prospect of interruption.

She wasn't particularly happy about this party, although it was in her honor. Papa should have known
how tired she would be. Shore commitments were always tough in the middle of an important racing series. Few sailors enjoyed them. It was totally different
from the way a crew ached to unwind after the whole
thing was over.

She hadn't left the marina until five-thirty this afternoon, with sunburn beginning to sting on the back
of her neck where the collar of her jacket had worn
the sunscreen away. Her eyes had ached from the
glare, her whole body, steeped in salt water, was beginning to chill, and her ears had been scoured by the
wind. She had soaked in a hot, fragrant bath for almost
an hour, then had had to scramble to dress in time to
greet the first guests at seven.

At least tonight was a little more casual than last
night's big event at the Evans mansion. She wore
loose silk trousers and a matching camisole top, the
patterned fabric splashed with vibrant colors inspired
by traditional Andalusian designs. Her hair flowed
down her back, concealing the sunburn, and her
makeup was very simple.

Spike-heeled shoes, which clung precariously to her
feet by means of a couple of thin straps, were her only
concession to high fashion, and they already hurt. She
shifted her weight, trying to get comfortable, as both
she and Holt watched her father's approach in silence.

He didn't just meander across the room, he moved rapidly and with intent.

"You're wanted for an interview," he said as soon as he reached her. "Two journalists from the American Spanish-language press. One is from a women's magazine. They're both very interested in your new role, and how you balance your priorities. Here, I meant to give you this upstairs, but there wasn't time. You should have it for the interview. Quickly now."

"Papa…?"

His fingers began to thread something around her neck. "Lift your hair," he ordered. "I can't manage the clasp. There. Now the bracelet."

Only now could she see what he had given her—a necklace and matching bracelet of warm yellow gold, set with smoothly polished carnelians the color of Beaujolais wine. Each piece was beautifully crafted, clearly the work of a master jeweler and worth a small fortune.

"Papa?" she said again, lifting her face. She brushed the curve of the necklace with her fingertips. It was cool and heavy against the fine skin that stretched across her collarbone.

Holt muttered something under his breath that she didn't catch. He wiped a hand around his neck and looked away, as if something was making him suffer.

"You deserve it," her father said. "Now go. The journalists are waiting in my office. They've been fed. Give them what they want with their questions. It's good publicity for us."

He nudged her in the right direction with a firm hand in the small of her back, and she went, still able to hear Papa behind her saying, "Now, Holt, my

daughter is not the only beautiful woman here tonight.''

The journalists kept her for forty-five minutes. It
was almost farcical. The male journalist was from a
boating magazine, and the woman represented a magazine with a major emphasis on celebrities, glamour
and lifestyle. Papa should never have scheduled them
together. The two were an impossible mix, and ended
up taking turns with their questions, while quietly
seething at each other.

Marisol was asked about her necklace, about *Skyrider*'s keel design, about her love life, *Skyrider*'s sail
wardrobe, her beauty regime, *Skyrider*'s crew, her favorite clothing designers, *El Duende*'s chances in the
Laser-class solo... It went on and on, and she finally
called a halt to it as politely as she could.

''You must have plenty to work with, now. I'm not
sure what more I can say. I'll look forward to reading
the articles.''

Her head ached, and she felt as if she'd been split
apart like a cooked lobster.

''Thank you, Senorita Villoria,'' said the woman
from the celebrity magazine. ''This has been wonderful. Of course we'll need photos. Could we arrange a
session tomorrow? Would you wear the necklace and
bracelet?''

''If I could just ask about the sail you blew out
today?'' the boating journalist said.

Papa appeared in the doorway. ''All done? Good,
because there are some people you need to meet, Marisol. Important clients. Tidy your hair and please remember to smile.''

She pasted one onto her face at once, in case later

on she forgot. Her cheeks ached, and the sunburn on her neck stung harder.

An hour later, Holt said to her, "You look like you could use some downtime. I fixed up a couple of supper plates for us outside. Meet you out there, okay? By the pond? Your dad's busy right now. He won't notice."

Marisol lifted her face to speak, but found herself bereft of words. She felt as if she'd used up her full quota of speech tonight and had nothing left. Holt seemed to understand.

"Relax your face, sweetheart," he told her softly, "or it's going to crack."

His hand brushed lightly along her jaw and was gone again before she had time to react. His touch soothed and cooled her skin like an expensive lotion, and her legs felt like rubber.

"Thanks," she managed at last, and skirted the edges of the crowded room to slip outside.

Holt went to join her a few minutes later. She didn't hear his approach at first. The splash of the stone fountain that flowed into the ornamental pond masked the sound of his footsteps, and he was quite happy about that. Wanting some time to think about what he was doing here, he stalled for a moment on the steps.

Okay, so he was attracted to her. That was no big deal. He was an athletic and red-blooded American male and he met women he was attracted to all the time. But this felt different, and he didn't know why.

Because it was such a surprise after the way he'd felt about her at sixteen? Because she was a competitor, and this added a thread of danger that appealed to his hunger for riding the edge?

Or was it because their attraction—he knew she felt it, too—was something he could use?

She looked wrung out after her long flight just two days ago and the nonstop commitments she'd had ever since. Fernando was so tough on her, spoiling her like a princess one minute and parading her like a winning prizefighter the next. Most women would have thrown up their hands long ago and said, "Enough!"

Marisol hadn't, and Holt knew it wasn't because she was under her father's thumb. She loved her life. She loved to race. Many of the women Holt dated wouldn't even set foot on a sailboat. Those who did only wanted to hang out on the deck, sip champagne and work on their tans. The stripped-out interiors of modern racing boats, bereft of any luxury, appalled them.

It suddenly occurred to him that he shouldn't blame his dates. The fault was in him. Why did he go out with women who weren't happy around boats? Could it be that he was protecting himself in some way, giving himself an excuse to avoid deeper involvement and virtually guaranteeing that every woman would bail out as soon as the initial excitement waned?

Unconsciously, he whistled a sigh of frustration between his teeth and Marisol heard him. She looked up.

"I'm watching your supper plate, Holt," she said. "The hot food is getting cold, and the cold food is getting warm. Come. Sit and eat. What are you doing, standing there?"

"Wondering if this is how you look in your garden in Spain." Having found one of the easy answers that were his specialty, he came down the steps and sat beside her. The garden was empty but for themselves.

Any guests who wanted fresh air tonight would go out to the patio on the opposite side of the house, fronting the water.

Marisol laughed at his words. "We don't have a garden in Spain. We have an apartment overlooking the marina at Puerto Banus, and a house up in the hills in a town called Ronda, about twenty miles from the coast. It's nothing like this."

"Tell me what it's like, then."

He wanted to know more about her—what had made the changes in her, how she spent her time, how she felt about her family.

"Well, Marbella and Puerto Banus are crazy," she answered as she ate. "So many people with so much money to spend. You should see some of the cruising boats we build there! I mostly stay out of that scene."

"Mostly?"

"Not always," she agreed. "Sometimes it's fun to go clubbing with a sheikh's daughter, or to laze the day away on some huge cruiser with gold faucets and a solid mahogany bar, where I don't have to do any of the work."

"I can see the attraction."

Yes, and he could see *her,* in a French-cut white bikini with the top discarded, the way they did in Europe, her high, rounded breasts tanned and gleaming with oil in the sun, her hair piled up behind her head, on a lounging chair, the Mediterranean sun bouncing off her silver-lensed sunglasses and making her glossed lips shine. His groin tightened, and he shifted his supper plate to a more useful position on his thighs.

"More often," she said, "I'm the wild woman in

the bow of a racing boat, yelling at the motor-cruiser skippers to remind them that sail has the right of way. The marina at Puerto Banus has over nine hundred moorings, and it gets busy. My grandmother prefers Ronda, and so would I, if I didn't have so much salt water in my blood.''

''What's so nice about Ronda?''

''Not so many tourists up there away from the coast. Our house backs the El Tajo gorge, and we have steps going all the way down. The house is cool and quiet, and we go for walks and sit with our friends.''

''She's there now, your grandmother?''

''Yes, she doesn't travel anymore. She was sick before I left, or I would have flown over with the rest of the team two weeks ago to get acclimated and to train. She's feeling much better now.''

''But you're still jet lagged.''

''I'll be over it in another day.''

''And how is Diego?''

''Papa saw him this morning. He's recovering as expected, and feeling a lot stronger.''

''You didn't want to go?''

''Of course I wanted to! Diego and Papa would jointly have killed me, though, if I had. We had to drill our maneuvers all day.''

''Tell me the truth about you and Diego,'' he asked, dropping his voice even though they were completely alone. ''You hedged around it last night. I got the impression…'' He stopped, wanting her to say it herself, not wanting to put words into that beautiful mouth.

''Is it your business?'' Her black eyes were slightly

narrowed as she looked at him, and the angle of her jaw was like a challenge.

"I'm trying to find out if it might be my business," he answered. "If you're serious about him, I'll back off."

It was the first time he'd admitted, to her or to himself, that there was another option, that he was interested. His words created a thick aura of danger and awareness in the air.

Her gaze didn't fall, and her chin stayed where it was, high and neat and strong. "And if I can't tell you that, yet?"

He dropped his voice. "Maybe I can help you to make up your mind."

Okay, now she looked down. She was uncertain, and flustered. She hugged her arms across her front, and he saw the tiniest, downiest hairs on her shoulders rise as if she was suddenly cold. He wondered if those suntanned nipples he'd imagined earlier had risen, too.

"Don't flirt with me," she said, her voice pitched low. Her light accent licked at the corners of each word like flames licking paper.

Maybe I'm not. Maybe it's more than that, and I mean every word of it.

He didn't say it aloud. Didn't know if it was true.

"What should I do, then?" he asked instead.

"Talk to me."

She stood up, restless. Her plate was empty and so was her wineglass. She left them where they were, on the garden bench, and began to clip-clop along the path in her uncomfortable heels.

Her patience for the shoes had evidently run out. Shaking them from her feet, she picked them up and dangled them in her fingers by the straps. Her bare brown toes with their pretty, clear-polished nails stretched appreciatively on the cool paving stones, drawing his gaze.

He followed her, his gait not as lazy as he wanted her to think. "What shall I talk about?"

"Tell me about blue-water racing," she said. "Tell me how it feels to be two thousand miles from land, halfway between New Zealand and South America."

"You're talking about the Whitbread, but that's not the scariest race I've done. The 1998 Sydney-to-Hobart was far worse."

"You raced the Hobart that year? The year of the storm?"

"In Australia they called it a storm. In Florida we would have called it a hurricane. The forecasts and the computer weather models we had access to before the race were way too cautious, and it hit our boat on the edge of Bass Strait like Christmas in July. We lost our mast, and the hull delaminated and started to break up."

"*Madre de Dios!* I've heard a few stories about that race, but I'd like to hear yours."

"I got winched from seventy-foot seas into a rescue helicopter about two minutes before the boat went down. Fifty-five other people from a slew of other boats needed the same thing over two nightmare days. Six men died, although none were from our boat. I kissed that paramedic rescue swimmer who hauled me in, I can tell you!"

"Those guys are pretty tough," Marisol agreed.

"This guy was sure tough—and she was a woman. A rookie. Her first live rescue. She'd been working on

helicopters for just two months. She was incredible!''
He shook his head. 'There were guys who'd been sailing for thirty years, who'd sailed that race a dozen
times, swearing they'd never do it again.''

"And you?"

He grinned, almost embarrassed about it. What did
this say about him? That he was a hero? Or that he
was crazy? "Did it again in 1999, and twice more
since.''

"You got back on the horse."

"It's what you're supposed to do. Pitting yourself
and your boat against the elements is part of the
sport.''

"It still makes you tougher than a lot of people.
You don't show that side of yourself very much, do
you? It's not what the gossip says about Holt Evans,
that he's tough. Twelve years ago, too, you made it
look as if you'd never raised a sweat.''

"Twelve years ago, I hadn't," he answered honestly. "Got a wake-up call after some skinny little girl
beat me in a race.''

They were talking about it at last.

That race.

He knew it was time.

"I'm still skinny, Holt," she said. "Watch what
you say.''

"Skinny?" His voice went hoarse suddenly. "Hell,
no, you're—" He stopped.

Beautiful.

Breasts like ripe fruit. Legs as supple as kelp.

This wasn't what he needed to tell her. He knew
what he had to say. "I'm sorry, Marisol. I can't remember exactly what I said to you that day—"

"Oh, *I* can!" She reached out to a lush, tropical plant and began to shred one of its big, shiny green leaves with her neat fingernails, as if she'd hardly noticed what she was doing.

"—but I know I was a total jerk. Is it too late to apologize?"

"Why, do you think you ruined my life?" She started on another leaf, turning it into fringe. She was staring at it, but didn't even see it.

He stepped closer. "One look at you, and I'd have to be a fool to think that."

Another leaf trembled beneath her destructive fingers.

"Stop," he whispered. "Stop, Marisol. Leave the plant alone."

His hand closed over hers, chafing it. He couldn't believe how smooth her skin was. She spent as much time as he did winding winches and pulling on ropes, but it didn't show. She took care of her hands. He ran his callused thumb over her knuckles, then stretched it to the knob of bone on her wrist. He could circle her wrist with his fingers until they met his thumb and still have space to spare.

Yet she was strong. Her forearms. Her shoulders. He used both hands, brushing them lightly up her arms so that he could feel the contours of honed muscle beneath the warm silk of her skin. Her lips parted, and she watched him, lashes half screening her eyes.

His thumbs brushed her collarbone, shifting the gorgeous necklace around her throat. To look at her, you'd have thought she was her father's pampered princess, her role purely ornamental, her mission in life no more complicated than to score herself a high-profile marriage.

But the strength at the heart of her belied all this. Within, she was made of fire and steel, and he wanted to find that hot core in her soul, explore it and make his mark upon it.

He touched his fingers to her full, parted lips, then slid the fingers away and replaced them with his mouth before either of them had a chance to think twice about what they were doing. As mouth touched mouth, something surged inside him that he couldn't remember ever having felt before.

Six

Marisol gasped at the touch of Holt's mouth on hers.

It was velvet and hard heat. It was steel and silk and sea salt and sweetness, all rolled together. She felt as if she'd been overturned into the ocean and didn't know which way was up. She felt blinded by darkness and dazzled by light. She felt lost in a wilderness and found by a prince.

It frightened her.

A heaviness at once began to pool low inside her, an ache that was both intense pleasure and insistent pain. Holt stroked her face with those callused thumbs, muttering hot-breathed apologies against her mouth for his roughness, when he didn't feel rough to her at all. She loved the strength in his fingers, the sensual friction of his touch, and the press of his whole body against her.

She couldn't breathe, but breathing didn't seem important anymore. The only thing that counted was the taste and touch of his mouth, but Lord, did it frighten her!

She'd never been kissed with such confidence or such depth before. She'd never risked this nakedness of passion. Diego's occasional kisses of greeting or farewell were almost fatherly. With the nature of their feelings for each other still unclear, he never permitted himself to touch her mouth.

She'd dated junior Villoria crew members a couple of times as well. Several seasons ago they'd employed a Norwegian named Lars, but he'd left to join a British crew preparing for the Admiral's Cup. And the season after that, the son of a local Russian millionaire had raced with the team for a few months.

Both of these men, however, were too aware of her father's potential disapproval and its consequences. Their attempts at lovemaking had been snatched and tentative. They were waiting for Marisol herself to give them the cue to be bolder, but she never had. Her body had never led the way. She'd slept with Lars because she'd thought that was what you did after you'd been seeing each other for a while, but she'd never seen stars.

Holt was different, and so was everything about the way she responded to him. If he felt a particle of ambivalence or doubt about his response or hers, it didn't show.

Is it so very obvious that I wanted this? Marisol wondered. *It must have been....*

If it hadn't been at first, it was certainly obvious now. Her shoes slipped from her fingers unnoticed and dropped to the ground. She curved her hands over his hips and slid them back, claiming the tight, muscular shape of his *culo*. She enjoyed the sense of possession, the force of her touch.

He did the same to her, roving across the thin silk of her clothing, making her panties ride higher so that the pulsing heat between her thighs felt even tighter.

She glimpsed a universe she'd seen before only in

dreams—a universe she passionately yearned to enter
and explore. But once she did enter it, there would be
no turning back. She knew this about herself with an
instinct that had never troubled with words. It was
pure, intuitive understanding.

If she abandoned her body to him...

Her blood would catch fire.

Her spirit would belong to him forever.

Her heart would break.

Holt anchored her against him and she was left in
no doubt that he was aroused. Sliding his mouth from
hers, he buried his face in her hair. "Smells so sweet
and fragrant," he muttered. "Like orange blossom.
Satin against my skin. I can't believe it, Marisol. I
can't believe what you're doing to me."

His lips touched her neck, pressing like a brand,
and she threw back her head and gasped. His warm
breath flowed into the valley between her breasts, and
her furled nipples peaked harder. Every inch of her
body throbbed.

He slipped his hands inside the waistband of her
silk trousers and stroked her cheeks where her panties
had ridden up. At once, his fingertips found the sensitive creases at the tops of each thigh. She arched
back, wanting his mouth lower on the slopes of her
breasts, wanting to feel him taste and suck and caress,
but then she felt a sharp pinch of pain at her temple.

"My necklace," she gasped. "It's caught in my
hair and it's pulling. No, yours, too. Your hair."
Those long, silky-clean blond strands on the top of his
head, which she'd begun to thread her fingers through.
"We're tangled together."

Holt lifted his mouth from the slope of her breast

and tried to pull away, but stopped when he heard her hiss of breath. "Still caught?"

"Yes."

"I'll hold still."

In a way, this felt more intimate than their kiss had been. His cheek was pillowed hard against her breast, and she could feel the puff of his breath warming her skin. Carefully, she unthreaded the black tendrils of her own hair from the tiny claws that held each gem of the necklace in place. Even taking it slowly, she still had to break several strands.

Holt's hair was shorter and easier to pull free. Just as she untangled the final strand, she heard footsteps grating on the stone steps leading down to the fountain.

"Marisol?"

It was her father. Holt straightened at once, just as Papa came into sight, but no one was under any illusions. Marisol's disarrayed hair, Holt's twisted collar, their breathlessness and the awareness on their faces... It was obvious what they'd been up to, and they knew it. Holt had his hands thrust deep in his pockets, and Marisol's heart rate had only just begun to slow.

Papa made no mention of the thick atmosphere. "Do you know what time it is?" he asked her, after acknowledging Holt's presence with a short, sharp nod.

"You're going to tell me, I expect," Marisol replied. "Around ten?"

"Eleven. No one has seen you. If you can't do your duty as guest of honor—"

"I did, Papa! For two and a half hours!"

"—then you could at least go to your room early, so that you're well-rested for tomorrow. You have your solo race in thirty-six hours."

"I know that, Papa, and I'm very clear on my priorities."

"That remains to be seen," he answered. "Some of Tuesday's racers can afford the occasional distraction. You cannot."

Because you're a woman.

Marisol knew this was what he meant.

"Don't forget that," he finished.

"I'm not. I don't want to talk to anyone else tonight, but I'm quite ready for bed. I'll slip upstairs and you can make my apologies, if you like. You've been very happy to tailor my performance according to your requirements this evening. Why not bring down the final curtain, as well?"

"Marisol, don't overreact."

"Fine. You're right. I won't. Good night!" She glared at him.

Papa muttered something, turned on his heel and strode back up the steps. Only as she was about to follow him did Marisol realize she'd dropped both her shoes while lost in Holt's arms. They had fallen off the stone path and into the greenery, but were clearly visible. She bent down to pick them up, and straightened to find Holt watching her.

"I'll say good night, Marisol," he said slowly.

"Yes." She gave a distracted nod. "I'm sure we'll meet up tomorrow at the marina or on the water."

"Hope so." Just two words, and once again spoken slow and lazy.

A world of promise flashed into her mind like the

view from a speeding train. Her heart beat faster
again. To hide her response, she turned and ran
quickly up the steps, leaving Holt walking in the opposite direction behind her. The garden flowed around
the corner of the house toward a second set of steps
leading up to the side of the terrace at the front. He
had chosen to go that way.

Suddenly, she felt the same loneliness she'd experienced out on the water today when faced with Renaldo's hostility. Pressure. There was too much pressure. She could handle the demands of racing. She was
sure of that. It was in her personal life that the stress
was making cracks.

She had seen the expression in her father's eyes. He
didn't want her in Holt Evans's arms. He wanted her
with Diego. He wanted her settled in Spain, pregnant
with a son and happy to give up racing, happy to
substitute her own ambitions for those of her husband
and her child.

Did Holt have to deal with any of this?

No! He was the Evans family's golden boy, and
always had been.

But maybe the problems she faced at home made
Marisol tougher. Maybe she needed every bit of this
maddening opposition in her life to firm her own de-
termination to win.

Was Holt aware of any of this? Was it possible that
he was just like her father and thought he could make
use of the fact that she was a woman, eliminate her
as a viable competitor in the races by distracting her
with sex and romance? Men had used women that way
through the ages, and Holt was far too smooth to let
his hidden agenda show.

''I should tell him straight out that he's wasting his time and mine!''

Turning to yell at him right now, she saw him walking up the front steps, clearly visible through the gaps in the shrubbery. Even from this distance, she could see the expression on his face. It was preoccupied and thoughtful, as if he had questions on his mind as well.

Why confront him now? she decided with a cooler head. Actions spoke louder than words, in any case. She had nothing to prove to Holt Evans face-to-face. She could prove everything she needed to on the water.

Inside the house, she could hear that the momentum of the party was still high. Her sister-in-law, Consuela, was a fabulous hostess and often helped Papa with his social obligations. Pausing, she almost went through the double doors and into the main reception room again. There were people she hadn't spoken to yet, and whom she'd like to see. She had let both Papa and Holt monopolize her for far too long.

But the thought of the coming races pulled her toward her bedroom, via the rear staircase that climbed just beyond her father's office. She wanted to drive to Miami to see Diego in the morning, and the crew had a long session of practice on the water scheduled for the afternoon. She needed to spend an hour or two with navigational charts and weather models to shape her thoughts on strategy for Saturday's blue-water clash with the other maxi yachts.

Thinking about all this as she came along the corridor toward the stairs, she heard voices spilling from Papa's office. The door stood slightly ajar, the light was on and Papa was in there. She heard the tail end of a terse comment from him, and then her brother Juan's voice.

"You know why Diego suggested her, Dad!"

Marisol froze, her shoulder pressed against the corridor wall and her toes, still bare on the thick carpeting, just out of reach of the finger of light which extended through the open door.

"It's not because he thinks the team can win with her in charge," Juan went on. "It's because he hopes that is the best way to get her up the aisle and into his bed—not necessarily in that order. The man is weak where Marisol is concerned. As if the way to win a woman's heart is to give her what she wants! It's the opposite!"

"You're right about what Diego wants," Marisol heard her father say. "And I hope it will happen."

"Don't let your hopes blind you, Papa."

"It's all right. I'll speak to Renaldo, if necessary. In reality, the crew can take their orders from him. He won't let her make any big mistakes."

"Is that good enough?"

"I hope so. You're right. Perhaps I shouldn't have listened to Diego on this. I must tell him this isn't the way to win her around."

"He should be firmer with her."

"If she fails too badly in practice and in the solo race, I'll put an end to this farce, put my cards on the table and let everyone know that Renaldo is formally in charge."

Marisol felt as if her chest might burst, and the blood rushed to her head. She hurried past the door to Papa's office on silent feet and didn't stop until she had reached the safety of her room, where she paced as if she was imprisoned there.

"I am so sick of this!" she whispered.

Even a whisper hurt her constricted throat. There was a taste like vinegar in her mouth, and her temples throbbed. She would have cried, only she was too angry for tears. She would have stormed back down the stairs and yelled, only if she tried to speak—to Papa, to Juan, to Holt, to *anyone*—she would sob so hard she might choke.

"What does Papa want from me?"

She fumbled with the clasp of the beautiful necklace he had given her tonight, and pulled it from her neck. It felt like a bribe, or like a silly trinket used to distract a child from the forbidden goal the child wanted much more.

She tried to take the bracelet off as well, but her fingers were so clumsy in her anger that she couldn't manage the clasp. She tried to drag the ornate gold links over her hand, but even when she folded her thumb as tightly across her palm as she could and scraped white scratches on her skin with the bracelet's sharp edges, it wouldn't fit.

The bracelet felt the way Papa's love felt tonight—genuine and valuable, but like a fetter far more than a gift.

"What the *hell* are you trying to do to your daughter?" Holt's voice was tight in his throat and hard with the force of his anger. He'd felt compelled to follow Marisol, in order to make a definite arrangement about meeting her tomorrow, but that would have to wait.

Fernando Villoria and his eldest son looked up from

some business papers they had spread across the desk, their mouths falling open a little. They hadn't heard Holt's approaching footsteps on the deep pile of the carpet. On the hardwood floor of the office, his feet were louder. He entered the room fully and slammed the door shut behind him with a kick of his heel.

"What did you hear?" Fernando growled. He slid the fan of papers into a single pile. A brief glance told Holt that they were financial spreadsheets related to the Villoria boat business. He had no interest in them.

"As much as Marisol heard," he said. "I was behind her. She didn't see me. Just as the two of you didn't see her."

"And both of you are happy to listen to conversations that don't concern you, apparently," Fernando said.

"It *does* concern me! And it sure as hell concerns her!"

"Yes? It concerns you? Think about that, Holt. It's a bold claim. You want her to win?"

"No! But I want our boats to beat the Villoria boats in fair races. Which they won't be if she has another crew member undermining her position. A team can't work that way. There has to be trust."

"You're very honorable in your outlook all of a sudden."

Holt ignored him.

"Your daughter is good at what she does, Fernando," he said. "You should believe in her. And if you don't, you shouldn't pretend otherwise. Trying to live up to what you want from her must be like walking on quicksand. Hell, *I* wouldn't like to be in her position!"

"What on earth are you talking about now?"

"Let her, at least, make her own choices about what her heart wants. Are you really happy to push her into a marriage with a man who has a serious heart condition and who is more than twenty years older than she is? I guess you are happy, when he's your right-hand man and that allows you to extend your control over her even further."

Fernando laughed. "If you think I control Marisol, then you don't know my daughter! You think it's about control? It's about Diego, and the fact that he's a good man. His heart condition has been treated now. Better an older man, a steady man, than a man of her own age who is never going to grow up."

"Meaning me, Fernando?"

This was a battle of two forceful wills. Juan was enjoying the spectacle, Holt could tell. His black eyes glittered, and his mouth was tucked up to one side in an amused smile. Holt didn't feel nearly so relaxed. He recognized Fernando's strength of personality, his shrewdness, his ruthlessness.

Fernando loved Marisol. He wanted the best for her. In Holt's eyes, he had a strange definition of "the best," but that didn't mean he'd put anything less than his whole soul into getting it for her. He would make a dangerous enemy—and a scary friend.

"You brought a date to your family's party last night," Fernando said, still without taking his eyes from Holt's face. "Tonight, you're putting fire into my daughter's face and a wild look in her eyes. She wants you. And don't forget that I live here in Emerald Cove for much of the year. I know your reputation. I know how many other women have wanted you, and how casually you've used that. If you pursue my daughter, you had better have something very different in mind."

"I realize that," Holt growled. "I'd be a fool if I didn't."

"And are you so sure you're not a fool, Mr. Evans?" Fernando Villoria said.

Holt dropped his gaze.

The man had a point. With women, his track record of commitment and longevity wasn't great. What did he really want with Fernando Villoria's daughter?

"She has gone to her room," Fernando said. "I suggest you don't follow her. You should give yourself some time to think." His tone was sheathed in gentleness, like a lion's velvet paw.

"I'll do that," Holt answered. "But trust me, sir, there's some thinking you need to do, also."

"Juan?" Fernando said.

His son nodded and stepped to open the door. Holt's cue to leave. He took it without regret.

The door clicked shut behind him, and at once Fernando and Juan begin to talk about business matters. "I won't have time to deal with any of this, Juan," Holt heard. "Now or for the rest of the week. I need to get back to the party, and I need to be available for Marisol when she needs me."

What about me? Holt wondered. What am I prepared to give Marisol, if she needs me?

He pushed through the party crowd, which had begun to thin out a little. Juan's brother Luis, younger by a year, was doing duty as host with his incredibly beautiful Venezuelan wife. Honey-blond, with perfect teeth and an even more perfect figure, Consuela was

the kind of woman Holt had dated often—the kind
who mistakenly thought that her beauty was enough
to make her interesting.

Mostly, Holt had begun to realize, it wasn't.

Marisol was different. He knew that. It was a no-
brainer. Beautiful, strong, skilled and so very alive.
Dating her would be nothing like dating anyone else
in his experience. Was he up to the challenge? And
the responsibility?

He said his goodbyes to Luis and Consuela, found
his parents, whom he'd accompanied here, and fobbed
off their questions as to what he'd been doing with
himself for the past couple of hours.

"I'll walk home," he said. "I need some air."

And he needed to think about Marisol. He'd kissed
her tonight, and the touch of her on his skin still
seemed to burn. Was kissing Fernando's daughter the
best thing he'd ever done? Or the biggest mistake of
his life?

He couldn't envisage, with a woman like Marisol,
that there could possibly be any middle ground.

Seven

Could this be Holt Evans walking past along the waterfront?

Yes, it was.

Renaldo Tejerizo recognized the gold-blond hair, the broad shoulders, the confident strides, even in darkness. Not that you could call this blue-and-silver night backdrop true darkness. Compared to the inky black of a cloudy, moonless night in his native village in Spain, Emerald Cove's waterfront was as bright as day.

Renaldo possessed a blue-water racer's sharply-honed night vision, and the splashes of spilled light everywhere made him uncomfortable. If Evans saw him, or, worse, someone from the Villoria crew...

He stepped into the shadow of the Clipper Bar's service entrance, putting a critical three feet of extra distance between himself and the stranger he was talking to. He doubted that Evans had seen him. The man looked as if his mind was a thousand miles away.

"I need some time to think about this," Renaldo said.

The answer came back immediately. "Twenty-four hours." The stranger blinked and peered, as if his own night vision wasn't nearly as good now that Renaldo stood in shadow. "I can't give you more. You seize this chance or you lose it, Tejerizo, it's very simple."

"You're saying this is an opportunity?"

"What else? Aside from the up-front payment I'm offering—which is generous, as I'm sure you'll agree—there are the ongoing benefits to your career. Villoria has treated you shamefully, and your crew can't possibly win any of the important races with a woman in charge. The team I represent will value your abilities far higher."

"How?"

"With the Evans maxi in fragments and Villoria disqualified through its implication in the sabotage, you can rest assured we'll make certain your hand is not evident in this. We know what we are doing. The way will be clear for my crew to win with ease. Imagine yourself skippering an America's Cup challenge a couple of years from now. As a member of my crew, that is not impossible."

"You keep saying that," Renaldo cut in. "'My team'. 'My crew'. Who are you? You haven't told me. You've given me no facts at all. Who is it that you represent? *British Blue?* The *Omega* team?"

"Do you really think I can tell you before you've committed to this? Please show me that you understand the way these things work, or I'll doubt your capacity to pull it off."

"That is *not* in doubt," Renaldo growled. This man made his hackles rise. On the other hand, much of what he said made sense. Villoria *had* treated him shamefully. And he hated to lose. "The only thing in doubt is my involvement. As I said, I'll need to think."

"And as *I* said, you have twenty-four hours. We'll meet here tomorrow night—" The stranger paused to cough, and Renaldo heard the whistle of an asthmatic wheeze in his breathing. "And you will convey your decision."

The man turned to leave without even waiting for Renaldo's answer. Again, this irked him deeply. "But if I need to contact you—" He still wanted more. Information. Leverage. Straight answers.

The man turned back and smiled. He had something hidden in his hand. A pocket-sized asthma inhaler. Renaldo's youngest sister was asthmatic, and he recognized the gray-blue mouthpiece of the inhaler jutting from the end of the stranger's closed fist.

"You will not need to contact me," the man said. "Please stop insulting me with your assumption that you can trap me into revealing facts you don't need to know. Concentrate on your opportunity, and on deciding whether or not you're man enough to take it."

Renaldo swore under his breath in Spanish, then shrugged. "Tomorrow night, then. *Generous* was the word you used, wasn't it? You'd better spend the interval wondering whether your offer is generous enough. Otherwise I'm not the only one wasting my time."

Yes, I'm sure I can get a bit more out of him, he thought a minute later as he entered the Clipper Bar, his dry mouth craving a Mexican beer.

"Lookin' good," said the dark-haired nurse.

She slid her fingertips from Diego's wrist, where she'd just taken his pulse, and ripped apart the Velcro that fastened the blood pressure cuff around his arm.

"Are you sure you got it right?" Diego teased. His black eyes twinkled, and he looked so much better than when Marisol had last seen him two days ago. "Hadn't you better take it again, just to make sure?"

"Sorry, honey, I've heard that line before," the nurse answered. With a severe face, she jotted some figures on his chart, put it back in its holder at the end of the bed, capped her pen and slid it into the breast pocket of her uniform.

"But you haven't heard it from me."

She relented and smiled at him. A woman somewhere in her mid-forties, she had a pretty smile and a pretty figure, amply endowed. "True," she said. "I haven't heard it from you, and you deliver it better than most."

"Naturally. I'm a Spaniard," he murmured.

"The cute accent helps, too," she answered, and left the room, still smiling.

"It's so good to see you smiling, Diego!" Marisol said after the nurse had gone. She reached out and squeezed his hand.

"That nurse is not so hard to smile at. There are a couple of dragons, who keep trying to tell me what I can't eat. Which seems to be practically everything."

"You'd better listen to them, get well and get out of here. We need you, Diego. We miss you."

Very carefully, she didn't use the word *I*. Such a little word, but it would have suggested too much, promised too much.

Diego had most definitely been flirting with that nurse. Marisol tested her feelings on the matter, the way she'd have tested a sore tooth with her tongue. Did it hurt to see the way he'd softened Nurse Meiklejohn, to note the way the other woman had begun to sparkle at him?

No.

It didn't hurt at all. The only thing she felt was relief, because it proved how much better Diego was feeling. Such a pity! It *should* have hurt. Jealousy would have been a welcome emotion. It would have flooded her with some of the same passion she'd felt last night—the rush of heat in Holt's arms, coupled with the anger she'd felt on overhearing Papa and Juan.

But it was never going to happen. She was never going to feel jealous of Diego's interactions with another woman.

He'd fallen silent. Looking up, she saw how closely he studied her.

"I've had a lot of time to think since Saturday," he said quietly in Spanish. "And a lot of reasons for a new perspective. It's wrong, isn't it? It feels wrong. The way we touch each other. The way we care for each other. I've wanted it. You've grown into such a beautiful woman, Marisol, and we have so much in common. But there's something missing."

"I know." She felt her color rising, but was glad he'd brought the issue into the open.

"Some spark," he went on. "A man and a woman need that *anhelo,* that *deseo,* that hunger for each other."

"Yes," she agreed. "You're right, Diego. That's what's missing. All of that."

Meeting his eyes, she was afraid that he'd see the longing and the desire he'd spoken of reflected in her face—the longing and the desire that she felt for Holt.

But he only shifted in his raised hospital bed, and asked, "How was your practice yesterday?"

Marisol began to breathe again. Her face wasn't as naked as it felt, apparently.

She hesitated before answering his question, sorting through her options.

We wrecked a sail.

Renaldo is verging on mutiny, and Papa will support him all the way.

Holt's boat beat the skin off *Skyrider*.

"Fine," she said. "It was great. The crew members you recruited here are slotting in well. We shaved some more time off our maneuvers. It went fine."

She stopped. Opened her mouth and took in a breath that wasn't steady. The words threatened to spill out.

But Papa only went along with your suggestion that I should captain the team because he's so keen for you and me to commit to each other. He's on the point of destroying my authority with the crew and putting Renaldo in my place, in reality if not in name. Renaldo's just about the only person of any importance who doesn't realize that, and so he hates my guts. And I have to ask you, Diego, did you only put me forward for the role because you thought that was the way into my heart?

"You'd better get back, hadn't you?" he said. "Practice this afternoon?"

"Yes. The crew's probably already working on the boat."

"So, go. Get out early. Every tiny bit of extra effort gives you more of an edge."

Just as he'd suggested, she went. Purely to make

sure she would keep her *boca maldita*—her cursed mouth—shut and say nothing of what she was thinking. She looked back at Diego from the doorway and saw that he'd closed his eyes.

He looked tired and older than his years.

"Way to go, team! Way to go, *Unicorn!*"

Two gorgeous blondes were standing on the dock shrieking in the direction of the boats, and it didn't take much effort to realize that they'd come to cheer Holt and his team. Mainly Holt.

"Where's the posse of bare-chested male models cheering *Skyrider*'s female skipper?" Marisol muttered.

She hoped the other women wouldn't see her as she scooted past them and leaped onto her own boat. This whole scene reminded her too strongly of high school here in Emerald Cove twelve years ago—her sense of isolation, her crippling shyness, her agonizing awareness that she was an object of ridicule to those who got pleasure from ridiculing others.

This morning she had raced home from seeing Diego, after getting stuck in traffic at the start of the drive. Her absence kept the boat from getting out onto the water. After bolting down a sandwich, a wedge of cake and a glass of milk, she'd jumped into the first clothes that came to hand—denim cutoffs, a Villoria team T-shirt and her oldest yachtie shoes.

Mindful of how her tan had faded while she'd looked after her grandmother indoors for two weeks, and how she'd gotten so burned yesterday, she'd slathered sunscreen on her face until she gleamed like a showroom car, and had emptied half a tube of mauve zinc cream onto her lips to keep them from chapping. Her ponytail was pulled through the hole in the back of her green Villoria baseball cap, and her black bra showed through the green-and-white shirt.

It wasn't exactly a cheerleader look. If there were still people around who enjoyed the opportunity to be cruel...

Again, the practice went badly. Renaldo was in a foul mood. Papa had come on board, supposedly to check the computer equipment, but really, Marisol was certain, to check her. The wind had dropped to-day—just the right breeze for the sail they'd shredded yesterday, which they hadn't yet replaced. The smaller spinnaker just didn't have enough surface area to catch the air, and the other four maxis on the water all left *Skyrider* for dead.

Renaldo demanded of her, "Why isn't the new sail on board?" and she realized it was indeed her fault.

She'd said yesterday that she would pick it up from the sail loft in Key Largo on her way back from seeing Diego in Miami. She'd forgotten totally. In the face of Renaldo's accusing stare, she almost lied and said that the sail wasn't ready, but her belief in the importance of trust and honesty between crew members won out.

"I forgot," she said, facing him squarely. "I'll pick it up first thing tomorrow."

"So this entire practice is pointless."

"No. There's a lot of other stuff we can work on. Drill our tacks and our jibes and our sail changes again."

But even that wasn't a success. Two of the youngest guys in the crew had had a heavy night in the Clipper

Bar yesterday, it turned out, and were feeling the effects. Jose Aguilera announced timings for each maneuver, and every one of them was slower than the times the crew had achieved the day before.

Marisol took her two hungover crew members below deck. One of them was Bjarne, the young Dane who'd cut his hand during Sunday's practice. His hand was still bandaged, but drew no sympathy from her right now. She eyeballed both men and said, "If you want to drink during a race week, find another boat. You won't get a second chance on this one. Clear?"

They both looked uncomfortable and told her they understood. As they clumped back onto the deck, Marisol was aware that, over by the nav station, Papa's focus wasn't on the computer as he pretended. He'd listened to the whole thing.

She resisted the temptation to look at him, to try and gauge what he thought of how she'd handled the crew, and went back up on deck herself.

Back at the marina at six o'clock, after they'd stowed the equipment and locked up the boat for the night, Holt was the first person she saw when she stepped onto the dock. He was heading away from the moorings also, his tan deepened by the afternoon sun and his hair blonder by contrast. Seeing her, he waited. She wished he hadn't.

"You needed the big spinnaker," he said.

"It's still at the sail loft." She didn't mention the fact that this was her own fault.

"Bad luck."

"We worked on other areas. It was fine."

"Don't take this badly, but you might want to consider—"

She stopped in her tracks and yelled at him. "If you're about to give me a sailing tip, Holt Evans, I suggest that you don't."

"Hey, I was only—"

"There's more than one way of turning this into an unfair fight, and I'm not interested. Okay?" She lowered her voice and repeated with less volume but far more intensity, "Not interested, Holt."

It was so far from the truth that she almost expected him to laugh out loud, grab her by the shoulders, pull her into his arms, kiss her silly and prove her wrong, then and there. To save herself—or maybe to save face—she didn't give him the opportunity.

He stood there while she strode quickly away, and she knew he was watching her.

What did he think? How much did he guess? He'd apologized last night for his behavior and his cruel comments twelve years ago. But had he forgiven her, at heart, for beating him that day? He had the jungle instincts of a born competitor. How far would those instincts take him? What was last night really about?

To her horror, some pent-up wall of feeling inside her burst open and she started to cry—tears of frustration and fatigue and stress that she just couldn't control.

Holt watched Marisol as she walked away. Her neat, curvy butt swayed inside her frayed and cheeky denim shorts. Her brown legs looked as long as a seabird's, and a heck of a lot prettier. He could see the black straps of her bra quite distinctly through the white back of her T-shirt, and though the green *V* at the front had been more opaque, it had offered the suggestion of some enticing contours and outlines while she'd yelled at him just now.

Despite her passionate Spanish blood, Holt didn't get the impression Marisol yelled all that often. It confirmed his sense of how much pressure she was under right now, as did the frantic way she was wiping the heels of her hands over her eyes. Damn it, she was crying!

Just ahead of her, he saw a male journalist, a second man with a huge black camera bag strung by a strap on his shoulder, and a fussily dressed woman who launched into a spiel in Spanish while Marisol was still fifteen feet away. Half blinded by tears, Marisol evidently hadn't seen their approach until now.

She clapped a palm to her forehead, and although Holt couldn't understand what she was saying, the gestures spoke for themselves. She was apologizing. She'd forgotten something. No, she was late. She still needed to change. A photo shoot, evidently.

Lord, as if she needed something like that now!

Breaking into a loping stride to cover the distance more quickly, Holt caught up to the group. He didn't waste time on niceties. Instead he said, "How about you leave her alone? Cancel. Reschedule. All she wants to do is have a shower and some food and take a break. Can't you see that?"

Marisol rounded on him. Her eyes were red and her nose was puffy, just as he'd guessed they would be, but her expression was fierce. "I can handle this, Holt. Go take your own shower!"

"I'm planning to," he answered.

"And don't try to run my life!" She turned to the young male journalist—he looked around twenty-three

years old, good-looking in a baby-faced sort of way—
and put on a smile that could have lit the whole of
Key Biscayne. "I'd be more than happy to give you
an interview," she said. "As you've just heard, I have
another commitment first. A photo session at my father's house. I need to change, obviously. Would you
like to meet at Amberjack at seven-thirty tonight, and
we'll do the interview then?"

Amberjack, Holt thought.

Damn.

Amberjack was Emerald Cove's most expensive
waterfront restaurant. He was eating there himself tonight. With Heather, whom he'd known in school. He
began to hope that the dollar amount in the journalist's
expense account was on par with the guy's age, and
therefore wouldn't run to a place like Amberjack. Apparently, however, the expense account was heftier
than he'd hoped.

"Miss Villoria, that would be perfect," the journalist said.

"I'll meet you in the lobby," Marisol told him, and
flashed him another dazzling smile—a smile that se-
gued effortlessly into a glare as her eyes turned in
Holt's direction.

"It's a nice restaurant," he murmured, hiding what
he felt. This was an old habit, and he'd gotten very
good at it. "Try the Florida quail."

Eight

Holt hadn't seen Heather Mathieson for about five years. Five years before that, they'd graduated from high school together.

A couple of weeks ago, she'd called him from Miami out of the blue, after seeing his picture in the sports pages of the *Miami Herald* and reading the article alongside it. She had been gushy on the phone, talking about how wonderful his success was and how great it would be to catch up on old times. She was coming home to Emerald Cove for a weekend soon, coincidentally, and she'd love to get together, if he was free.

Heather was high-maintenance. Amberjack was really the only choice. She'd taken his suggestion as her due, and he'd made a reservation for eight.

Marisol and her journalist were in the middle of their interview and just starting on their appetizers when Holt and Heather were shown to their table. To Holt's critical eye, it didn't look like a very professional interview. For a start, the journalist did all the talking. Marisol had her chin cupped in one hand, while the other hand fingered her wineglass. Her neck and shoulders showed an uneven tan. Her eyes were bright—dreamy and shining, exotic and beautiful.

The journalist would be crazy not to mention those

eyes in his article—and if he *did* mention them, Holt would probably want to kill him.

Marisol said something at last. Unfortunately, Holt's table was too far away for him to hear what it was. But he *could* hear that both of them were laughing. Matching, harmonious laughs.

Heather said something. He had to get her to repeat it, and even then he couldn't summon much interest. Vehicle colors? Her dad was giving her a Mercedes sports coupe for her birthday, and she couldn't decide between white and red. What did Holt think?

"Red," he answered automatically, and he thought of Marisol and the red dress she had worn two nights ago. Marisol and the wine-colored stones of the necklace that had caught in their hair as they kissed. Marisol and the crab-stuffed sweet red chili pepper she was biting into right at this moment.

"White is more classic," Heather answered. "I'm leaning to white right now." She giggled. "I change my mind about twelve times a day."

Well, it's always good to have a hobby, Holt thought, and realized that he was intensely bored.

Or he would have been, if he hadn't had Marisol to look at in the background. His eyes strayed in her direction constantly, and Heather wasn't *that* self-centered. She noticed.

Eventually.

She twisted around in her seat and studied Marisol casually for a moment, showing Holt her bare and flawlessly tanned shoulders in the process, then asked, "Who is she?"

"One of the racers. Spanish. But she went to school

here. You might even remember her. Marisol Villoria.''

''Ohmigosh!'' Heather squealed, clapping both palms to her cheeks. ''I don't believe it! *That* is the Lobster Queen?''

Holt choked on a mouthful of beer and gulped it back quickly. ''The what?''

Heather giggled again. ''We used to call her that. She blushed like a cooked lobster every time someone spoke to her. She was hysterical. I don't believe that's her! If you like that type, she actually looks almost pretty.''

''People change in twelve years, Heather.''

''Not always,'' she trilled.

''No, not always,'' he agreed. ''Some people don't change at all.'' His voice had an edge, and his agreement didn't count as a compliment to his date.

Since Heather had hardly touched the meal she had ordered, and looked horrified when he suggested dessert, he took her home as soon as he decently could. Marisol and the journalist had just asked for more coffee.

''You can come in,'' Heather invited as Holt's car sat idling in her driveway. ''My parents are out tonight. Real late, they said. And anyhow, I have my own wing and it's a long, *long* way from theirs.''

Her meaning was more than plain, and if Holt had been in the slightest doubt, the husky, suggestive tone would have clarified any confusion. Right now he found it hard to imagine how a man could be less interested. He made up some smooth excuse about his race schedule tomorrow, and she backed off immediately.

Kissing him sweet and fast on the mouth to let him know just what he'd missed out on, she told him, "Don't walk me to the door. I'm a big girl. I can find it on my own."

Holt arrived home by ten.

Way too early.

He prowled the house like an animal, unable to get Marisol out of his mind. Had she invited the journalist back to her place? Holt didn't think for a second that the man would have turned down such an offer.

He didn't waste any more time on pointless speculation as to what Marisol could be doing at this moment, nor on an analysis of his own state of mind. He got back in his car and drove to her place to find out.

She met him at the door, still wearing the little black dress she'd worn at the restaurant. He didn't know if she was alone. How could he tell? She stood with her beautiful, willowy body blocking the doorway, and she wore an expression of imperious hauteur and disdain that could have belonged to a seventeenth-century Spanish princess in a painting by Velázquez.

"We need to talk," he said.

She raised her black eyebrows and cocked her head to one side. The Spanish princess way of saying, "Oh, yeah?"

Two knots of muscle tightened on each side of Holt's jaw. He tried again, swallowing the body blow to his ego that she seemed to deliver so effortlessly with such simple weapons. "Okay, correction, *I* need to talk."

She looked at him for a moment, her black eyes impossible to read. "Not here," she said.

Holt heard her father's voice in the background.

"Wherever you want," he agreed. "As long as we're alone. We could take a walk to the marina. It's a beautiful night."

She nodded and disappeared, leaving the door open just a chink. He heard her speaking in Spanish, way too fast for him to make out the few words he might have known. Her father replied, much more briefly. Marisol spoke again, more hesitantly this time, and Fernando Villoria said, "Holt?"

"*Sí!*"

She didn't wait for her father's response, just snaked her way through the doorway and closed the door behind her.

"I need to be back by eleven thirty at the latest," she said.

"Your father still gives you a curfew? At twenty-seven?"

"It's my own decision, Holt, not my father's. I want a good night's sleep. I'm racing tomorrow. And so are you."

They walked in silence toward the marina. There were some other people about—tourists mostly, enjoying the magic of the cove at night. Lights reflected on the water. Ropes made music against the masts. It was the perfect time and place to kiss a woman, but Holt had already picked up the very definite vibe that that wasn't going to happen if this particular woman had her way.

They reached the guarded end of the marina, and he pulled his security pass from his pocket and flashed it at the bored-looking security guard. Marisol didn't have hers with her, but it didn't seem to matter. Maybe she gained entry purely on the strength of her smile. Holt wouldn't have been surprised.

Instinctively, he headed for *Unicorn,* a dark, silent shape, skirted in tarpaulins, up in its cradle. It would receive its final coat of the experimental hull finish tomorrow, right here in the dock, while the solo races took center stage.

"Why are you angry with me?" Holt asked Marisol at last.

No subtlety tonight. No flirting. Serve it up raw.

"I'm not," she answered. Her teeth were clenched, and she didn't walk beside him, she walked one pace ahead.

He laughed. "Sure, you're not!"

Immediately, the fire in her flared. "Why did you come to see me if you knew I was angry with you?"

"Because it bugs me when I'm attracted to a woman and something's getting in the way. Like anger. *Your* anger, Marisol."

"I don't think we should be having this conversation. I shouldn't be here with you. I don't need this complication."

"Who says it's complicated? It isn't! It's simple, Marisol. It's so damned simple!"

Her turn to laugh. The sound had an edge. "How can you possibly say that?"

"Stop." He reached out and planted a hand on her swaying hip. She felt warm and alive, and she moved like a smooth wave rising in front of his boat. She didn't slow down. "Stop, and I'll show you how."

He swung himself in front of her and she had no choice but to stop short, in the shadow of the maxi yacht. Her hips mashed into his upper thighs, and her lower stomach pressured his groin. He kept his hand right where it had skidded to a halt as they both stopped moving—on the firm curve of her bottom. It felt as if it belonged there, just the way his mouth belonged on hers as soon as they touched, and his fingers belonged in the silk of her hair.

She did nothing to push him away.

Yes, he was right and she was wrong. This was so simple, a three-year-old child would have understood.

She still tasted faintly of chili—exotic and fiery and sweet. Those three words fit so perfectly to describe Marisol herself, and he felt as if he'd be able to taste her, feel her, on his lips forever. Her response was so intense and heartfelt that it made his head spin. He'd never known quite such a sense of triumph and pleasure in bringing a woman to such a level of heat, and so fast. Despite anything she'd said, she wanted him as much as he wanted her, and he fully intended to make her admit to it in words.

He kissed her more deeply, nipping her lower lip gently with his teeth, parting her mouth with his, tasting her, drinking her, running his hands up her sides until he felt the swell of her breasts, holding their weight in his hands and thumbing her nipples, circling around them so that their peaks hardened and jutted into hot beads.

It wasn't enough. Still, he wanted words.

"Talk to me, Marisol. Tell me why you're still here if this isn't what you want. Tell me why this isn't as simple as it feels."

She didn't answer, just chased his mouth, cupped her hands around his face and pulled him close again. She had her eyes closed, as if she might overload her senses by keeping them open. He wanted to see those black eyes, to learn the way they clouded and pooled and blurred when she felt his heat.

At the same time, there was something so intoxicating about the blind rapture in her face. Her lashes feathered against her flushed cheeks, and her lids were creamy and thick, with a crease in each one like a stretched-out, sideways S. The creases emphasized the exotic shape of her face. He kissed each lid, felt them flutter beneath the touch of his mouth, kissed her temples and her earlobes and her neck.

Her dress scooped low at the back, and he couldn't believe how soft her skin felt. Each knob of her spine was like a velvet-covered button, and her nape was as sensitive as a butterfly's wings. Breath hissed between her teeth when he touched her there, and her lips, already swollen from kissing, fell open. The tip of her pink tongue pushed out between her teeth and he chased it and caught it with his own, deepening their kiss still further.

Finally, he dragged his mouth away. "You never answered," he said. "You never gave me a reason. You can't tell me why this isn't simple, can you?"

"No," Marisol agreed unsteadily. "You're right. I can't."

She tilted her face downward and buried her forehead in his shoulder. She had to grip him hard to keep her balance, the way sailors gripped the rail in heavy seas.

"I want to go further with this, Marisol. When do you fly back to Spain?"

"Monday. A week from today."

"That soon? You can't stay longer?"

"My grandmother worries about me when I'm away, and I'm concerned about her health. Her chest hasn't quite cleared yet. She's so independent. My sisters-in-law can't always get her to look after herself the way she should."

"So we only have six days."

"Six days for what, Holt? That's the real question."

Marisol felt his hesitation and his uncertainty in the brief, flinching tension of his body, before she heard it in his low-pitched voice. "I don't know for what." He loosened his hold on her, but his touch was just as powerful when it fell more lightly on her body.

"Then you'd better work it out, hadn't you?" she said. "Both of us had."

"Tell me what part of it you think is in doubt."

"Whether I can trust you."

"*That?* You doubt *that?*"

"Almost as much as I doubt the wisdom of trusting myself. I've seen you with two different women in just the three days I've been here, and still here I am in your arms, the next in line." Her accent tangled the sounds of the words, belying her almost native fluency in Holt's language. "I'm not sure which of the two of us looks worse in the light of your reputation, Holt. You for trying to turn me into another notch on your belt, or me for letting it happen."

"I don't look at women that way," he told her. "I don't. Heather Mathieson called me, I didn't call her. And when she asked me in for coffee tonight, and made it pretty plain what was on the agenda, I didn't go. You *know* I didn't go. You know what time I left the restaurant and what time I got to your place. And on Saturday, I didn't even get to take Tori home."

"I'm sure you'd find a good reason to discount all the rest of them, too—if you could remember all their names."

"Is that really what this is about? How many women I've dated?"

"It's about whether I'm content to be next in line. Can you honestly say, Holt, that you're promising the possibility of more than that? Six days, or even six months. Am I in any way different?"

It was so close to what Fernando had challenged him on, Holt realized. And, so help him, he didn't have an answer yet. He'd spent the whole of his adult life protecting himself from the need to give more. He'd saved everything—his strength, his fight, his commitment—for racing.

And if, at the end of a weary day, there was a little bit of energy left unburned, he gave that to his family. To his parents, Russ and Lynn, who were so proud of him. To his brother, Seth, who used him as a sounding board a little more often than Seth would want to admit. To his sister, Laura, who was serious and hard-working and who had been a little lonely until her marriage last month.

Until Holt had seen Marisol again, three days ago, he'd have sworn there was no room in his life for anything more than what he already had, and that he was happy this way. Now he wasn't so sure.

But how could he say this to Marisol, when he had no idea yet exactly what he was offering and how far this might go? She was different, but what did that mean? How could he put both of them under this much pressure?

He couldn't.

Still holding Marisol in his arms, he felt her stiffen and saw that her attention had been caught by something a distance away, just beyond the marina's guarded entrance.

"Is that Renaldo?" she said, half to herself. "What's he doing here this late? Is there a problem with the boat?"

Holt laughed. "He's a sailor, isn't he? He's checking the charts, checking the course, checking the equipment, checking the weather. Like we should be doing, since we're not in bed and fast asleep. Obsessing about the races should be our only excuse for being out this late."

"This late? Is it—?"

"Almost midnight."

She narrowed her eyes and shook her head. "What's happening to me, letting you do this? Falling for this stuff?" Immediately, she began to walk away from him, toward the shore.

"Takes two."

"No." She shot a sideways glance at him and her eyes sparked with black fire. "No, it doesn't. Sometimes it only takes one. I shouldn't have let you—I shouldn't have come out tonight. What have we proved? That we lose track of time in each other's arms. Nothing more. There's nothing else between us but physical chemistry, Holt. And that, as I'm sure you could tell me from your own experience, is not a significant thing."

"Don't," he said. "Don't make the chemistry into a reason to feel bad."

"About you?"

"About anything. I can understand that you want time to think about what's happening. I'll walk you home."

"No, thank you."

"Your father will—"

"I'll ask Renaldo." She turned in the direction of the Clipper Bar. "Papa will be only too pleased to have Renaldo walk home with me—a man he can trust! I'll see you tomorrow, when we race."

"Starting line, maybe," he drawled deliberately. "Not at the finish. I'll be way ahead."

She laughed. "I'm glad you're so sure of that, Holt. It will make it more satisfying to prove you wrong."

She quickened her pace and walked away, waving her arm in the air and calling, "Renaldo? Renaldo, that's you, isn't it? Can you walk me home? Tell me what you think of tomorrow's forecast."

Yeah, I'd like to know a little more about what's in the forecast myself, Holt thought as he went through the security check-point and turned in the opposite direction.

A storm warning for his heart. High pressure on the home front. The winds of change and regret blowing from all points of the compass. And a woman in his life who was as complex as *Unicorn*'s computer navigation system, and as hard to handle as a rudderless boat in a forty-knot gale.

He wondered if Marisol would reward his understanding and hard work as much as his boats did. And he wondered how flattered she would be by the comparison with an inanimate object made of carbon and fiberglass and metal and rope.

* * *

Renaldo wasn't alone.

Marisol didn't realize the fact until she got closer. There was a second figure standing beside the service entrance of the Clipper Bar—a man who must have been positioned deeper in the shadows when she'd first caught sight of her fellow crew member heading in that direction. He and Renaldo had finished their conversation, apparently, because the man disappeared around the corner of the long building before Marisol reached Renaldo.

"Who was that?" she asked. She heard a high, wheezy cough, cut off abruptly. The man had probably gone into the bar.

"From another crew," Renaldo answered. "We were discussing the weather. Come on, you wanted me to walk you home, didn't you?"

"Well," she drawled, "Papa would want you to."

"Your father's right. You shouldn't walk home on your own at night. You shouldn't be out this late at all. And not with Holt Evans."

Knowing he was right, she said nothing. Renaldo stalked ahead of her like a belligerent bull, saying nothing also. She felt like a naughty child, skipping to keep up with a stern parent.

I could let it go. How likely is it that Renaldo and I will ever see eye-to-eye on anything?

But then she rebelled. She wasn't in the habit of admitting defeat so easily.

"Listen," she said, catching up to walk beside him, determined to match her pace with his. "I understand that this isn't easy for you, and—"

"Stop. Don't say this. You don't need to."

"I want to, Renaldo. We can't work this way. We certainly can't win this way."

"What are you suggesting?"

"That we try harder. Both of us. To find a meeting point. To swallow our differences. I want to win as much as you do."

"Are you questioning my loyalty? Because if—"

"No. No, I'm not."

"Then there is no need for this conversation to continue."

Not knowing if her attempt to reach out had made things better or worse, Marisol left the subject alone, and they walked in silence to her father's house.

Solo racing had been Holt's first love. No friction between egos. No one to depend on but himself. Tuesday morning was filled with a program of junior races, and he stayed away from the water, wanting to keep his mind fresh.

Seth had work for him to do.

"Pretend you're from the navy."

"Aye-aye, Cap'n!"

"This is serious. I want to run a dress rehearsal on the computer demonstrations we'll be making on the weekend. Play devil's advocate for me. Sit and watch the computer screen in my office while I go through it. Hit me with the hairiest questions you can think of on budget and performance and flow-chamber stats and everything else. We need to be three jumps ahead of every argument the navy might use to say no to buying this sub."

Two hours later, at company headquarters, Holt told his brother, "I'm buying the Stingray sub. In bulk. I don't care how much it costs. I'll have a scale model for my bath tub, if necessary. Your case on the benefits of this technology is very well argued, Seth, as far as I can see. Congratulations!''

Seth winced. ''Wait before you open the champagne, okay?''

''Hey, you're really stressed out about this, aren't you?''

''We've invested a lot of time and money. We've stuck our necks out. I'm hoping we haven't put those necks right on a chopping block.''

''How could we have done that?''

''This business of Rebelian spies going all out to steal the technology is spooking me. The navy has given us their weapons specifications to integrate with the sub's operating system. That's top-level security. If we were responsible for that information leaking out, the whole company would be crippled by the fallout, not to mention the implications for national security.''

''I guess I hadn't thought about it in that light.''

''You know, when we first found out that our own cousin, Marcus, was one of a family of genetically engineered children with extraordinary powers, I felt...honored, I guess, but also—'' He stopped.

''You saw it as an opportunity, right?'' Holt guessed. ''You looked at what Evans Yachts could get out of it?''

''Exactly. Not in a bad way. I mean, this is a business. You use the assets you've got. Nothing underhanded about it.''

''But you're having second thoughts?''

''I'm thinking I was pretty naive. Like it or not,

we're a target, now, and there's no turning back. Marcus and Gideon and the others have been living with that reality for a while, but I'm only just seeing it. Maybe we never should have gotten involved with the Stingray.''

"From what you've said, it's going to be the best craft the company's ever produced."

"What's the cost going to be, Holt? Emerald Cove is crawling with people I've never seen before in my life, and every single one of them looks like a covert operative to me. If a six-year-old kid squeezed under the fence in our backyard after a runaway basketball, I'd probably handcuff him first and ask questions later."

"Relax, Seth!" Holt engulfed his brother in a hug, and then, in case that was too touchy-feely, he punched him in the arm. "Trust your instincts on who's with us and who's not. And remember, you're not alone. Meanwhile, I'd better get to the boat."

"Win for us, Holt."

"I intend to." For sentimental reasons, if nothing else. All his early wins had been in small, around-the-buoys solo races like this one.

An hour after he'd left Seth, and with a meal under his belt and all his gear checked, Holt sat alone in the Clipper Bar and drank mineral water for twenty minutes, getting his head ready for the race. He could see the marina from the window, and found that, once again, there was a disproportionate amount of interest in Marisol and her boat.

Knots of people milled around her when she arrived at the marina, and seasoned yachties discussed her in the bar. Holt found it intensely irritating to hear the way people talked. Someone said he "knew for a fact" she used steroids and had failed a drug test a few months ago. Someone else was equally sure that her father was an arms-dealing billionaire whose boats were purely a sideline and a way to indulge his spoiled daughter's whim to sail.

Thinking of Marisol's utterly feminine and non-steroidal body in his arms, and of the way Fernando, his brother, his sons and his father before him had worked their guts out for more than fifty years to build their business, Holt almost felt ill.

"Did you see the way *Skyrider* trailed the other boats yesterday?" the first voice said behind him.

"I've heard the crew aren't even speaking to each other."

How many of these guys can I take out before I'm arrested? Holt wondered. And could I post bail in time to get back here for the race?

His fists actually tingled, and watching Marisol as she climbed aboard her boat with onlookers still crowding her, he was so close to barging down to the dock and bodily throwing everyone out of her way....

Only he'd done something very similar yesterday afternoon, and for his pains had ended up watching her flirt with another man for half the evening.

He had a sudden flash of realization that made his head spin.

I want her to win.

He actually wanted to see her center stage at the post-race press conference. He wanted to see the triumph and happiness on her expressive face. He wanted to see her implacable, whip-wielding father wearing an aura of ill-concealed pride. And he wanted to come up to her, when the fuss had died down, put out a hand to engulf her long, cool fingers in his and say, "Congratulations, Marisol. That was a great win."

Was she that good? Would it happen?

He was convinced it was more than possible.

Great race conditions, Marisol thought. The wind came from the right direction for two sides of the triangle that formed the course. Now that she was clear of the dock, she at last had some peace. The onlookers and the well-wishers and the nay-sayers had stressed her out with their persistence and their questions. At least the Villoria crew, her father included, had respected her stated need to be alone today.

Twenty minutes until the gun.

The boats had begun to move in on the start line. There was a big field of competitors, and the water danced and undulated, white sails gliding to and fro over it. It was so important to time the start correctly. Too slow, and every other boat made it over the line first. Too fast, and you breached the line before the gun and lost agonizing time when you were forced to circle back and start again.

Ten minutes until the start gun. A cracking boom rang out across the water from the ten-minute gun, to alert the racers to the time remaining.

Different racers chose different risks. The bolder ones flirted with the line and the gun, cutting it as fine as they could, their goal to cross the line as soon as possible after the start. Marisol took a less risky course, preferring to start well back, then power across the line at speed, even if she started behind the field.

Holt betrayed himself as one of the bold ones. This

didn't surprise her. He maneuvered for position at the front of the fleet, holding his boat back like a rearing horse. She couldn't believe how finely he cut the timing, nor how crowded was the section of water where he jostled for position. If he didn't get out in front right at the beginning of the race, the other boats would rob him of vital wind.

Okay, just a few minutes until the gun, now. At one edge of the fleet, Marisol knew she had the room and the freedom to let her sail fill with wind and build her speed.

The gun went off, and Holt crossed the line a scant second or two later. The two boats ahead of him had to circle back, and the boats immediately behind him looked in imminent danger of a collision. He'd gotten the start he'd wanted. Marisol felt happy with her own position, also. She'd crossed the start late, but she was moving fast and had clear water in front of her.

Steering slightly to starboard, she would quickly close the gap between herself and the leaders. Maybe even come out ahead. It was going to be fast today, and her light weight compared to most of the other competitors should translate into an edge to overcome her lesser strength. There were other women in the race, but she knew they didn't have her experience, and she didn't expect any serious female rivals.

The only rival she cared about was Holt.

Could that really be true? Other competitors might beat her, but she realized—and it made her stomach drop uncomfortably—that Holt was the only one who mattered.

He cruised in front as they reached the first buoy, and Marisol lay in fourth place. Evidently a rivalry existed between the two skippers running second and third. Rounding the second buoy, they both tried to cut in too fine and sailed so close together that the right of way was debatable. Which was the leeward boat? Marisol heard yells of warning, then abuse, then a sickening scrape and crunch as they collided.

No time to see what had happened, or if the racers raised protest flags. Both boats were still afloat, with their skippers at the helm, but they'd lost a lot of speed. Marisol had to round the buoy herself now, wide on the approach, close in after the turn, and she needed all her focus for what she was doing.

It wasn't until she was running downwind, steady and fast, toward the final buoy that she had time to notice where she now stood in relation to the other boats. Holt powered along in front of her, but no one else. Another few minutes, and she had gained on him.

Then they rounded the final buoy and had to sail against the wind. The physical work required was much tougher, and Marisol felt herself beginning to tire. Strong male arms had the edge in this situation. She wouldn't overtake Holt now, although she was so close that she could see the sheen of sunscreen across the bridge of his cheekbones and nose when he looked back. She knew he'd have recognized her boat.

The finish loomed in sight. One more maneuver to refine her course and she'd have a clear run.

Into second place.

It wasn't good enough, but she couldn't do anything about it. She was sailing as well as she knew how, and as well as her strength would let her.

Holt made his final change of direction, and incredibly, he oversteered it a little, making the boat appear to brake in the water. Marisol overtook him, made her own maneuver and powered toward the finish. Holt's error hadn't cost him much time, and he'd already begun to gain on her again. The gap between them closed fast. She could hear the voices of people on spectator boats, yelling and cheering. She caught the blurred green and white of several Villoria team jackets. Was Papa among them?

She crossed the line.

In first place.

Holt skimmed across just seconds behind her.

The press conference half an hour later was a stress factor she could have done without. Papa claimed the focus of attention, with Marisol beside him. He wouldn't let her answer any questions herself, although she'd have preferred to do so rather than listen to the answers he gave.

"I never doubted the high standard of our Villoria boats. Our craftsmanship in construction and fittings is unmatched, and it shows. More importantly, I never doubted my daughter's ability to win. She has had my full support from the first, and that support has been vindicated today. The rest of the week will continue to showcase the dominance of our team in virtually every event."

He wrapped his arm around her shoulder, then lifted her hand high above their heads in a clench-fisted victory salute. When the cameras began to click, he thrust the winner's trophy into her hands and muttered to her in Spanish, "Kiss it and smile. Hold it up."

Marisol held her feelings in check until the press conference was over, then under cover of the noise as everyone began to leave, she demanded of her father,

"So, you've had total confidence in me all along? Does this mean I can stop wondering when the team captaincy will suddenly revert to Renaldo? Does this mean I can stop watching my back, waiting for the flash of the knife? What a hypocrite you are sometimes, Papa!"

"Not a hypocrite. A businessman. And, yes, a hard taskmaster. Answer me honestly, Marisol. Would you want this if you did not deserve it?"

She closed her eyes. Hot tears of exhaustion had filled them, and she came close to losing her strength completely. Holt seemed to have gone. They'd seen each other after the race, but crowds of people were in the way and they'd never gotten close enough to speak.

He'd given her a thumbs-up sign and mouthed, "Congratulations!" but somehow she didn't feel the rush of satisfaction she'd expected. Holt would have won, but for that final inexplicable mistake. If she hadn't known all about his competitive instincts from personal experience, she might almost have wondered if he'd...

No.

Holt would never throw a race.

So what had happened?

On top of all this, Papa's attitude made her feel as if she had weights on her shoulders, which she must carry while giving the impression of walking on the lightest feet in the world.

She wanted to yell at her father, "Yes, I *would* want it! For once I don't want the effort and the burden of having to 'deserve' something. I want your approval and your confidence just because I'm your daughter.

Just because you love me. I don't want any other issues involved.''

She doubted Papa would ever give her that.

''Go home, *querida*,'' he said. ''Take a shower. Lie down. Get Yolanda to scramble you a big pile of eggs for your supper, with hot toast and bacon, and go to bed early.''

He kissed her forehead and she opened her eyes. His face was as hard to read as ever, and even his final whispered ''You did well'' could not lift her spirits.

What if I *hadn't* done well? she wondered. What if I'd lost by minutes? Would he have kissed my forehead then, and talked about showers and scrambled eggs? I'd have worked just as hard. But would he have been proud?

Would *I* have been proud? I wanted to beat Holt so badly, and I did. So why do I still feel as if something's wrong?

Nine

"**M**arisol Villoria is *what?*" Holt called through the closed door of his private bathroom.

"Waiting to see you downstairs," repeated his mother, just outside.

Holt had a suite in his parents' large home, consisting of bedroom, study and bathroom, which made it easy for his well-meaning mother to act as his social secretary when she thought it was required.

"She looks gorgeous," Lynn Evans added helpfully.

Acting as his *overefficient* secretary, Holt amended inwardly.

"In a dark-red silk sheath," his mother went on. "Very close-fitting, with little straps. I would kill for that girl's figure and coloring!"

"Thanks, Mom," he called.

Like I needed to know that about the dress, while I'm standing naked in the shower.

He adjusted the faucet so that the water ran colder.

"Should I tell her you'll be right down?" his mother asked.

No, tell her it's going to take me at least fifteen minutes to get over the red silk sheath thing, and figure out what I'm going to say.

"Five minutes, okay?" he answered aloud.

"I'll ask if she wants coffee," Mom decided. "And where she bought the dress."

"In that case, I'll take ten."

Yeah, and what *was* he going to say?

He didn't know why the hell he'd done it. Call it an impulse. Call it empathy. Call it leverage. He'd deliberately maneuvered badly on the final leg of the race this afternoon to give Marisol the edge she needed to win, if she was a good enough sailor to make use of it. And she had been good enough.

Call it stupid, actually, because *she* was anything *but* stupid, and if she was here in his parents' house at this very moment…wearing a close-fitting red dress…

He turned the shower even colder.

…when she should be flaked out on her bed with a mud-pack on her face, it probably meant she'd worked it out.

He didn't think she'd be pleased.

It took him fourteen minutes to make it downstairs, and by then he'd decided on a simple strategy.

Denial.

And if that didn't work…

Nope, it had to be denial, because he honestly didn't have the words to explain the truth. He didn't know why he'd deliberately made that bad maneuver so close to the finish line. He'd never thrown a race before in his life. He'd never even considered the option. So why this time?

Holt heard Marisol before he saw her. She and his mother sat on a love seat, drinking coffee, in what the family had always called the ocean room. With its floor-to-ceiling windows overlooking the water, its spacious dimensions and its washes of bright color in decor and furnishings, the room had a dramatic quality, but this didn't prevent the aura around the two women from being exactly opposite.

No drama at all. They seemed as cozy as two kittens in a basket, and they were apparently conversing about fabric, to their mutual enjoyment.

Marisol turned when she saw him in the doorway. He caught the dazzling afterglow of her smile, but as soon as she focused on him, it faded, turning into a complex blend of questioning and thoughtfulness and vulnerability, and in that moment he understood exactly why he'd given her the edge today.

The realization took his breath away and made the blood start beating in his temples and his throat. His eyes pricked and stung, as if someone had just shoved a fist in his gut. It was scary, but it felt so right that he couldn't deny it for a second.

This was different. Totally and intensely different. What he felt about this woman, with her passionate nature, her strong body and her uneven tan, was utterly different to how he'd ever felt before.

She didn't look angry. She just looked tense, confused, full of questions she didn't know how to ask, and not sure why she was here. He understood all of this, and felt most of it himself. By instinct and habit, however, he hid everything behind the comfortable wall of his charm, went up to her and shook her hand.

"Congratulations on getting just the win your father was hoping for," he said. "I wanted to do this right after the race, but didn't get the chance."

His hand slid from her grasp too slowly, and the awareness between them sang like wind chimes in a breeze. The race had delivered an adrenaline charge that hadn't yet fully subsided in either of them.

"I know," she answered, a little awkwardly, blushing just the way she used to at fifteen. "I was hoping to speak to you after the race, too, but the marina was so crowded, and then there was the press conference. It was strange. Not the way I expected to feel." She frowned. "I wanted to ask you— Well, for a start, what happened to you just before the finish line, Holt? I—I really couldn't rest without finding out. That's why I'm here."

"What happened was no big deal," he answered lightly, far too conscious of his mother in the room. She had a built-in radar for any dishonesty on his part. On an impulse, he said to Marisol, "Listen, do you want to go grab something to eat while we talk?"

He wanted to talk, wanted to tell her what he'd just discovered about why he'd behaved so out of character today. He wasn't going to hide what he'd done. She needed to know. But in the right atmosphere, not here.

"Always takes me a few hours to unwind and slow down after a race," he added for his mother's benefit.

"Me, too," Marisol answered. She hesitated for a moment, then seemed to make a decision. "A meal would be nice. Could we go somewhere…" She closed her eyes for a moment. "…ordinary?"

He laughed. "You mean fast food?"

"Not quite that ordinary. But somewhere low-key, not at all fancy, and a little distance away, maybe, where no one will know us. Fine if it's crowded, just as long as the crowds aren't interested in *us*."

"Sounds perfect. Mom, I'm not sure if Dad and Seth needed me to—"

His mother waved her hands, which blurred in front of his vague, unfocused gaze. He was only interested in Marisol. "Go," his mother said. "They'll do without you. Marisol, honey, can I hold you to what you said about the fabric swatches?"

"I'll put some together for you as soon as I get home to Spain."

"There's no hurry. Bring them with you next time you come."

Holt watched in surprise as his mother hugged Marisol. Lynn Evans wasn't the air-kissing type and usually saved her hugs for the people she was close to. This was spooky. He recognized that the red silk dress had a powerful influence on his own state of mind, but didn't see why his mother should be similarly affected. He decided to get Marisol safely out of the house right away.

His mother, however, hustled them out the door as if this same game plan was all hers.

"What was that stuff about fabric swatches?" Holt asked Marisol as soon as they got outside. Talking about the race could wait. It was important, but it was also something he needed to get right and say at the right time. Fabric swatches were easier.

"Oh, we were just talking about Andalusian arts and crafts," she answered him. "I told her about our local leather and pottery, but it turned out she shares my passion for beautiful fabrics."

"She's had a very successful career as an interior designer, although she's very selective about projects she takes on now."

"Yes, so she told me. She's planning to redo the house, and I promised I'd send her some swatches."

"It sounds as if you know something about it." She also sounded cautious, as if she wasn't yet sure that she'd done the right thing by agreeing to come out with him. With a flash of insight, he realized that going all out to convince her on the issue would be the worst thing he could do.

Hold it back, Holt. Don't turn on the charm tonight.

"At one stage I considered opening a boutique here, featuring Spanish fabrics and furnishings," she said. "It's still something I may do one day. I can't race forever, and I love to be surrounded with beautiful things."

They drove to a busy Mexican bar-restaurant some miles away and found a welcome anonymity at one of the corner tables. Holt ordered margaritas, which were big, salty-sweet and cold, and they ate corn chips and guacamole and salsa, and shared a huge, sizzling platter of spicy shrimp.

Somehow, after a couple of hours, and a second margarita, they were still talking about a whole lot of things that had nothing to do with sailing, like beauty and family and life's simpler pleasures.

"From what I've seen," Holt found himself saying, "that's one of the best things about having kids—the way you rediscover the tiniest moments of wonder and happiness, flitting across your day like…like hummingbirds or something."

"That's cute!"

"My cousin Marcus's baby, Hank, can sit in his little baby seat just looking at his own fingers for minutes on end. I was watching him recently—and I thought, you know, he's right. He thinks it's a miracle that his mind can make his fingers move, and he's right. It is a miracle.''

Marisol watched him, sitting back in her chair. Her lips had parted in a smile and her eyes were soft.

''I feel a little silly, saying this stuff,'' he said to her. It was a far cry from the flirty conversations he usually had with women.

Marisol shook her head. ''No. It's good.'' She felt far more relaxed with him than she'd expected to feel. She added on an impulse, ''I think you don't show this side of yourself all that often, do you? It's so nice.''

''This is nice, Marisol.'' His voice had dropped. He took her hand and brushed his thumb across her knuckles, and her body started to heat at once, all the way through. ''This is incredibly nice.''

Even though they'd been in each other's company for over two hours tonight and had enjoyed every second of it, they hadn't talked about the race yet, as Marisol had burned to do when she'd first turned up on impulse at his house. They hadn't talked about sailing or boats or weather or the ocean at all, and it made for a refreshing change. Against her usual habit, she wasn't in a hurry to get to the subject.

Actually wanted to avoid it, if she was honest with herself. Her mind was on vacation, tonight. Talking about boats would have felt like a Monday morning alarm going off to awaken her in preparation for a job she didn't like.

This wasn't how she usually felt about sailing. Why was she feeling this way tonight? Why did she actively want to avoid the topic, as if it wasn't safe?

And why did she still feel as if today's victory hadn't given her the rush it was supposed to deliver? She let the questions go and seized hold of the subject of kids instead. Kids and families.

"Do you see yourself settling down someday, Holt?" Lord, now it sounded as if she was conducting a job interview! Her hand was still willingly imprisoned beneath his touch, challenging her judgment.

"I never use that expression, for sure." He grinned.

She understood his aversion to the phrase, and amended her question at once. "Okay, I guess I just mean staying in one place. Blue-water racing is like being a gypsy on the water, with the biggest races held all over the world."

"I love that. So many beautiful places. Sydney, Capetown, Ushuaia, the Irish Sea."

"But I sometimes wonder if that's why my dad took so long to accept that I wanted to race," Marisol said. "He was afraid I'd get hungry to go solo around the world or something and that I'd just never stay in one place long enough to have a real home."

"That was my recipe for heaven a few years ago— the sea as my only home," Holt answered. "But I guess deep down most of us know it's not forever. We do it, and no one can ever take away the achievement and the memories, and then eventually something else becomes more important and we leave that life behind. I'm not there yet, but it's going to happen. When Seth and Emma were nearly killed a few months ago, after the engine on Seth's catamaran exploded—"

"Exploded?"

"Accident," he said. "Pretty, uh, scary. There was a fire. They were lost at sea for a couple of days."

"Scary, all right!"

"And it made me realize just how important my family is. When their baby is born six months from now, I don't want it growing up knowing me only as a vague name because I'm never around."

"It's hard," Marisol agreed. "Spending my time in Europe, I hardly know some of my nieces and nephews, the ones who live here in Florida."

"You should fly over here more often. Hang on a minute, though." Holt frowned.

"What is it?"

"You said you 'wondered' if that was why your dad had taken so long to accept that you wanted to race. You mean he's never said? He's never talked to you about it?"

"Explanations aren't his style." Marisol shrugged and smiled, leaned a little closer, drawn in by the pull of Holt's touch. "He likes to have me guessing. It's another way of keeping me on my toes."

"And that's okay with you?"

"I'm used to it. I'm not going to waste my time on convincing him to change. I have more important battles."

Holt swore, with a single, biting syllable. He didn't apologize for it. Like Marisol herself, he wouldn't waste his time. He'd know she would have heard every possible curse, in half a dozen different languages, countless times on the water.

"My parents used to put my sister Laura—you know Laura—through similar stuff. But for different reasons. They weren't straight with her, the way they should have been, and it drove me nuts. What is it with parents of only daughters? Neither of you deserve that crap, particularly when you're both so strong.''

"You think of me as strong?'' Marisol couldn't help asking. She'd never applied the word to herself. Stubborn, maybe. Headstrong, as her father said she was. But strong? In a good way?

"I'm starting to think you're one of the strongest people I've ever met, Marisol.''

His eyes caught her in their warm light across the table, and she didn't know what to do or how to feel. The only man who'd ever looked at her like this before was Diego, and that had made her feel obligated and grateful as much as anything else. She'd never quite trusted the look, had never quite wanted it, and she hadn't wanted the similar looks she'd gotten from certain crew members in the past. Lars and Vadim, and others. But when Holt looked at her like this, she felt…real. She hadn't expected it.

"And you deserve—'' He stopped. "Hell, I don't know. Everything, I think.''

"More than I already have? My life is very close to how I want it, Holt.''

"Much more. More from your dad. More from me.'' His hand was still locked over hers. "You deserve the straight talking that your father won't give you, and I want to give it to you now.''

His fingers stroked the back of her wrist, sending currents of sensation jetting up her arm. She waited, knowing what he was going to say, afraid of it and wanting it at the same time.

"We've got five days,'' he said. "I don't want to

waste them. You know what's happening here. You told me yesterday that you didn't want to be the next in a long line. You're not. This is different. You know that.'' He revised the confident statement at once. ''I *think* you know it.'' The uncertainty convinced her more than the confidence did.

''I—I guess I *want* to know it,'' she answered him. Sounded silly, didn't it? Wishy-washy? He didn't seem to mind.

''I want to give both of us the best possible chance to work out whether five days is only the beginning. If that plan doesn't work for you, tell me now and I won't ask again. If it does…''

''It works for me, Holt.'' She could hardly get the words out. Again, he didn't seem to care. He watched her mouth as if her utterance had the power to stop a train in its tracks or shift the wind to a new quarter.

''Are we finished?'' he said. ''Do you want coffee? Or can we leave? I want to—'' his voice cracked ''—find somewhere and just kiss you crazy.''

''You can kiss me here.''

Both of them had already leaned even closer, like magnets to each other. Marisol loved Holt's honesty tonight, his mix of certainty and hesitation, different from his usual easy charm, and it seemed pointless to pretend she didn't want everything he offered.

''Here's not good enough,'' he muttered. ''Because kissing is all I could do. Somewhere else there'll be a lot more.''

''Kissing is a good start.''

''Kissing *you* is an incredible start. That mouth, Marisol.'' His was only a few inches away, now.

"Then do it." She smiled. "Step up to the plate, Holt."

What was happening to her? She never played games like this, never teased or used her sensuality with such overt, deliberate intent, but tonight she loved the new role.

"Whatever the lady wants," he murmured, and she watched through half-lowered lids as he angled his mouth, parted his lips and closed the final, electric inch of space between them.

His mouth tasted spicy from the shrimp and sweet from two margaritas. It was hot and firm and perfect. He took the kiss slowly, brushing parted lips across hers, nipping a little, deepening the contact with tantalizing precision. Marisol closed her eyes and let electric sensation wash through her like a warm wave. He was right. Kissing was nowhere near enough. She wanted his body heat, not just his mouth. She wanted his hands on her skin. And she wanted privacy.

When he muttered, "Let's go to my place," she didn't hesitate.

"Yes. *Yes!*" She sat back a little, breathless and already dizzy with need.

The sights and sounds of the crowded restaurant had blurred in her awareness, and she frowned as they came back into focus again. What an audience! Apparently no one had been watching, but it felt like an audience all the same. Stretching across to him as she'd done had dragged down the front of her dress, baring the upper slopes of her breasts to the chill of the air-conditioning vent just overhead.

Her father had persuaded her to dress up to go out tonight, even though she hadn't admitted to him where she was going. He'd found out about yesterday's encounter with the Spanish celebrity journalist, in her cutoffs and ragged shoes and he'd been angry.

"You can't afford to get yourself photographed that way! You shouldn't even possess such clothes!"

Okay, point taken, but she wished she hadn't chosen this figure-hugging, low-cut dress. She hugged her arms around herself, vulnerable in a way she hadn't been moments ago. Her instinct to suggest an anonymous location had been correct, but was it enough?

"I have my own entrance," Holt said, as if he understood what was going on in her mind. "This isn't going to hit the front pages of the *Envoy*, or anything. It's us. Purely about us and what we want. No one else."

She couldn't answer and just smiled, giving him her trust.

"I'll take care of the check," he said huskily.

They kissed again in the street outside, next to his car, and it was slower and sweeter this time. Deeper. More intense. His hand fell on her *culo* and he pulled her against him, then traced the curving line at the back of her dress where fabric and skin met.

"I want you so much it hurts," he whispered. "I'm shaking, Marisol. Let me just apologize right now, because we haven't said everything I wanted to tonight, yet—"

"I don't want to talk about anything right now."

"When we get to my place I'm going to—"

"Don't apologize," she whispered, and felt him shudder at the heat of her breath caressing his ear. "Just drive."

He did, taking shortcuts and flirting with the speed

limit all the way. He parked in the street, behind the car Marisol herself had left here hours earlier. She wasn't thinking anymore of the initial questioning impulse that had made her come to his house earlier. She was only glad that she had.

The Evans mansion was dark and quiet tonight, in contrast to Saturday's frenzy of elegant activity. Marisol didn't know who was around, and she followed Holt's lead in deciding not to care. He unlocked an iron-grille gate set unobtrusively into an angled section of the wall that fronted the street, then led the way down a secluded path before unlocking another door leading into the house.

In the distance, along a corridor, Marisol could hear a male voice—his father Russ, maybe—talking on the phone. As well, there was faint, canned TV laughter coming from somewhere else. No one was in sight, however.

A flight of stairs led to Holt's suite, where he had a bedroom and bathroom adjoining a study that contained a desk with a computer on it, easy chairs and a bar fridge. There was probably more—possessions and decor that revealed more about the private Holt Evans—only Marisol didn't have the time to look.

She didn't have the patience, either.

In any case, he hadn't turned on the light. As soon as he closed the door behind him, the room was bathed only in the blue light that spilled in from his large windows, facing the pool and patio. They went straight into each other's arms, impatience equally powerful in both of them. They wanted heat on heat, skin on skin.

Marisol slid her hands up inside his shirt, feeling

the hard contours she'd known she would find there—
lean, strong muscles, and ridged bone covered in
warm skin. His body was a sculptor's dream, a lover's
fantasy.

She felt her dress loosen and fall from her shoulders
as Holt found the zipper at the back and slid it open
in one movement, finishing just below the small of
her back. His fingers lingered there, discovering the
black lace of her panties. She shimmied her shoulders
and the dress dropped, slipping over breasts already
peaked with wanting. It pooled on the floor at her feet,
and she slid out of it, kicked it aside and stepped out
of her heels.

Holt stepped back, his breath hissing through his
teeth as he saw her. For the first time tonight she felt
self-conscious and uncertain. What would he think?
Her lacy underwear hid little. Were her breasts too
small? Were her nipples too dark? Was her figure too
athletic? Since her bra disguised virtually nothing, she
reached around and unclipped it at the back, just as
he disappeared beneath the shirt he was pulling over
his head.

By the time he flung it aside, her breasts were bare,
on show and waiting for his reaction to their shape
and their weight. He didn't keep her in doubt for long.
Stepping closer, he ran his fingers along the sensitive
folds beneath them, then dropped his hands to her hips
and his mouth to hers, pulling her close. Her nipples
brushed his chest, their sensitivity heightened by the
subtle contact.

"I've imagined you like this," he said softly. "Lying on the deck of a boat, wearing a tiny half bikini,

or slipping into the water, nothing but skin and sea. You're so beautiful.''

"So are you,'' she whispered. "Beautiful against my hands, and against my mouth.''

Reacting on instinct, not thought, she touched her lips to his chest, tracing the lines of his collarbone and pectorals with her mouth, learning the taste of his skin. He tensed and shuddered, and she wanted more.

"Take it all off,'' she told him. "This isn't fair.''

"You don't have it all off.'' The tease was intensely and deliberately sexual, coupled with his frank gaze at the single black triangle of fabric that still shielded her.

"That bit's for you,'' she said. "Whenever you want.''

"Maybe I don't want to take it off,'' he said, reaching for his belt buckle. "Maybe I'll just slip it aside when I'm ready.''

"Slip it aside with what?''

"My fingers. Or my mouth.''

The last word shocked her, although she'd angled for it brazenly. He intended to remove that last scrap of clothing with his mouth. She ached, just thinking about it, and felt impatience and need surging in her like a tide.

"Don't just talk about it, Holt,'' she said. Was that really her voice, as thick and sultry as the air on a hot summer afternoon? "Do it!''

"Hell yes, if we can even make it to the bed,'' he muttered.

They were already in a white heat. Holt cupped his hand over the triangle of fabric that tormented them both, and she knew how she must feel to him. Hot.

Wet. Ready. She rocked her hips against him in a movement that said, This isn't enough. One glance at the dark apex of his thighs as they tumbled into his adjoining bedroom told her he'd reached the same point.

She stretched back on the bed. Its handmade log cabin quilt was still in place, but neither of them cared. Marisol arched her back and writhed as Holt slid the fabric across her heat, just as he'd promised he would. His fingers and mouth took turns to work their magic. His breath was like a shock of electric current on her skin. She panted, sensitive to the point where pleasure almost became pain, and pushed him away so that she could pull her underwear down her thighs and kick it free. Even such a tiny barrier was too much.

He couldn't believe her impatience. "You're ready?"

"Yes. I'm sorry. Is that too soon?"

"No! I could bury myself in you right now, but I wanted to be sure this is what you want."

"This is what I want," she said. "And I want it now."

She took hold of him and steered him straight to her pulsing heat, then waited through long seconds of unbearable frustration as he reached for the drawer beside his bed, yanked it open, ripped a square packet clean across and sheathed himself.

At last! Shock waves ripped through them both as he came to her and slid into the lock of her opened body. She held onto him as if he were a life raft in a storm and moaned. The friction of his chest against her breasts knotted and tightened her insides like rope and she raked her fingers down his back until she could cup his buttocks and hold them hard.

His breathing was heavy and ragged, climbing in intensity just as hers was. They moved and breathed together, moaned together, swam into the hot darkness together. Her universe shattered seconds ahead of his, and they came back to earth at the same time. Slowly. Breathlessly. Speechless with the intensity, speed and power of what they'd experienced. Marisol took his head in her hands and kissed him with a wild mouth.

She kissed his hair and his temples and his nose and lips and eyes. She didn't need to say thank you and please hold me and I want to feel like this forever, because the kisses said all of it better than words ever could.

"Wow!" Holt said. "I guess I should come up with something better, but... Wow, Marisol."

"I like wow," she said.

"Gets the message across?"

"Yes."

"I'll say it a couple more times then." He did, and then they lay there in silence for several minutes. Marisol listened to the gradual slowing of his heartbeat and his breathing, and felt as if time had frozen in the most perfect moment of her life.

"Awake?" Holt asked in a creaky voice at last.

"Yes. Just...suspended, or something. Not sleepy, though."

"No, me neither."

He rolled onto his side and pushed up on his elbows, and she turned to meet him, feeling her still tingling breast pillow against her arm. His eyes looked very dark and serious in the dim light. Not playboy-blue and bright, but deeper, more thoughtful and more intense.

"Let's make some plans," he said. "Ready for that?"

She laughed. "No. Not yet. But I'm wondering if I'll ever be ready for it. I could lie here forever, I think. No, go ahead. Make plans."

"Let me kiss you first."

"Okay."

The kiss lasted longer than they'd intended. Much longer. Probably around an hour longer, because they were both in a much slower mood this time. No impatience. A different kind of hunger. Detail, rather than the big picture. Exactly how did it feel when they touched each other like this? Kissed each other like that? They whispered to each other, laughed a little bit, got taken by surprise when their climax flooded out of nowhere and washed them away.

They both slept, wrapped in each other, until Marisol's arm went numb and Holt woke up as she rubbed the feeling back into it.

"Okay?" he asked.

"Getting there. You cut off the circulation."

"I'm sorry. Can I kiss it better?"

She laughed. "Something's telling me that isn't a good idea."

"You're right. It could get us into more trouble. Can we work out when we're going to see each other? We have to get practical."

"I guess." She didn't want to. Not at all. So far, they hadn't had to work at this, and it made such a refreshing change for her. Making love was a kind of vacation, she discovered, a piece of perfect time that shouldn't have to end.

"You're not racing tomorrow, are you?" he asked.

Racing. The subject they hadn't touched on for hours. It made Marisol tense at once, without knowing why.

"No, but I have to be there," she said.

"How come?"

"There's a practice scheduled on *Skyrider* in the morning." She explained reluctantly. "And then in the afternoon there's a boat called *Clairette* racing in the classic yacht event. She was designed and built in Scotland in 1905 by William Fife." Marisol knew Holt would recognize the name of the renowned boat builder. "Villoria was commissioned to restore her three years ago after she was found rotting in some little port in France."

"Nice job!"

"It was. It's great to see her getting back to her former glory. Now she's owned by an American millionaire, sailing out of Chesapeake Bay. This is her first big public showing, and he wants it to be an event."

"So you're the official Villoria eye candy, are you?" He stroked the sensitive skin that ran from her armpit to her hip, and both watched as her nipples furled at once, wanting and remembering.

"Something like that," she answered, dragging her focus back with difficulty. "Papa thinks this guy has well and truly caught the classic yacht bug and is going to be looking for more boats to restore. He wants the work to come to Villoria, whether it's here in Florida or in Spain."

"Evans does good yacht restoration."

"Will Evans have official eye candy at the classic event tomorrow?"

"Uh, I doubt it."

"That would be Papa's point, I think." She grinned.

"Are you happy about it?"

"I'm not eye candy. You know that. And I love classic boats. Their beautiful lines and their polished timber."

"Mmm, speaking of beautiful lines…" He caressed her again, and she had to plant a hand on his hip to anchor herself. Another minute of this, and they'd both be set adrift again. "You're right," he agreed, still teasing her. "Evans Yachts should have representation at the classic event. I'll tell Dad I'm happy to do it. Who knows? There might be a couple of people who've caught the classic yacht bug, looking for a place that does good restoration, and we might get the work."

"Don't," she said, jolted out of a dream she didn't want to leave.

"What?"

"Remind me that we're in competition. Not just us, but our families, and our family businesses."

"Friendly rivals?" he suggested.

"Is that possible? Should we have talked about this before?"

"We all recognize that there's room for more than one player in the game, don't we?"

"You've always been such a consummate competitor. Can you really recognize that so easily?"

"I did today. I went out of my way to draw attention to the fact that there's more than one player in the game.'' He delivered the line with a flourish, still grinning at her, then immediately shut his mouth hard, and only opened it again so he could rake his bottom teeth harshly across his top lip. His sudden silence lasted long enough to give Marisol's stomach time to cave in, and he frowned.

''What do you mean, Holt?'' she said.

''I was going to tell you tonight, but not like this,'' he answered slowly.

''Tell me what?''

''About this afternoon. I thought you might have guessed. When you turned up here earlier.''

''Say it,'' she ordered him through gritted teeth. Her body had begun to tingle again. But for a different reason this time. She hated it already. ''Just pretend I'm not all that perceptive. Just pretend I was completely taken in by your distracting performance as a star-struck lover tonight. Just pretend I know you pretty well in other areas, however. That I know how competitive you are and that it never would have entered my head that you could—''

''Okay. Okay.'' His voice was strained. ''Yes, I made that bad maneuver in the final leg on purpose. I wasn't necessarily expecting that it would be enough. I was gaining on you. But I just wanted to show—''

''You pig! You arrogant, despicable pig!'' Marisol scrambled off the bed and onto her feet. Holt lay there, strong and golden and beautiful, still so sure of himself, despite that one slip he'd just made. ''You mean you still thought you'd win!''

"I would have, against most people. The fact that you—"

"No. I don't want to hear this. I don't want to hear your rationalization and your complacency." She began a furious hunt for her clothing, wishing for yesterday's cutoffs, stretchy polo shirt and scuffed up yachtie shoes, instead of all this slinky feminine gear that required wiggling and shimmying to get into. "You condescending, shallow, self-important—"

"Hell, don't you see, Marisol?" He rolled to stand in one easy movement, ignoring his own nakedness as if it had not the slightest power to make him vulnerable. "At the time I didn't have a clue why I'd done it. It wasn't until later this evening, when I came into the room while you were talking to Mom, that I realized—"

"I don't care what you realized." She snapped her bra together at the back and reached for her dress. "It doesn't make any difference. I'm going home to apologize to Papa. He was right all along. I don't want anything that I don't deserve. I thought I did, but I don't. And to find out that I didn't deserve today's winning trophy... I'm going to throw it into the bay." She swallowed around a painful lump in her throat, and almost pulled a muscle as she yanked her zipper into position. "And the five-day deal is off!"

"Listen, Marisol. I care about you. That's what I realized tonight. That's why I did it."

"Do you really think that makes a difference?"

"It does to me."

"Then you've got a problem. I'm not a sucker for a charming gesture. And I'm not one of your airbrushed blondes, Holt. That's not what I want."

"I can see that. I'm sorry. I'm sorry if I—"

"I don't want your apologies. You should have seen long ago that it would have to be totally different between us if it was going to happen at all. And the fact that you didn't—" She stopped and shook her head, flooded with pointless remorse. "Why did I let it happen? Why did I let it get this far without asking myself a few basic questions first?"

"Because you wanted me," he pointed out softly.

"Yes, I wanted you. I barely thought beyond that at all. I must have been crazy!"

Ten

"Impressive performance, there, big guy," Holt muttered to himself in the wake of Marisol's angry heels clacking along the tiled corridor and down the stairs.

He wasn't surprised that she thought his timing was terrible. Why hadn't he told her the truth about her win before that explosive, urgent episode of lovemaking? He poked around in his mind for the answer, like poking in the murkiness of a flooded drain with a big stick in search of something lost.

Yep, the motivation was definitely murky. He'd wanted to prove to her what he was increasingly sure of himself—that their connection could really mean something—*before* he took the risk of getting her angry.

So he'd known she would be angry?

Yeah, he had. Of course he had.

What serious racer wouldn't be?

As she'd said herself, she wasn't one of his air-brushed blondes. If Tori had been in Marisol's position, she would have gushed and squealed about it. "You let me win? Oh, that's so *sweet!*" She would have taken it as her due, as proof of his feelings—feelings that existed at just the shallow level she wanted.

Ironically, she would have been wrong on both counts. It wouldn't have been her due, and it wouldn't have proved a thing.

Marisol was the one who deserved a little help, a little attention paid to her interests. Marisol was the woman he had feelings for. And that meant even though he understood why she was angry, he was angry too.

"Right back at ya, Villoria," he muttered.

Grabbing a towel from his bathroom, he wrapped it around his waist and headed down to the pool. It was late. After midnight. Everyone else was sleeping, but he knew he wouldn't be able to. Not yet.

He let himself silently out of the French doors that led to the pool patio from this wing of the house and dropped his towel on a reclining chair. He hadn't bothered with swim trunks. There was no one to see. In the distance, he heard the slam of a car door and the throb of an engine. Marisol's engine. The car roared off into the night, with an angry woman at the wheel.

His body still ached and thrilled with sensation after what the two of them had done to each other in his bed not very long ago. The warm water slipped over his skin like her hands, and his body moved through it the way his fingers had moved through the silk of her hair.

But, yeah, he was angry with her.

Powering back and forth, using a fast, economical crawl, it was anger as much as the memory of their lovemaking that he attempted to vent with his movement. How come she couldn't see what lay beneath his actions tonight and in the race? How come she couldn't see that she was the only competitor in the world he would have done this for?

That meant something.

Something good, only she wasn't seeing it. He thought she had seen beyond the careless veneer he used for protection. He thought they had both gone beyond the superficial stuff with amazing speed, but as soon as they hit the first hurdle, she'd gone right back to the old assumptions and the old barriers.

It hurt.

It felt like a slap in the face.

Did she think she was the only one who'd become vulnerable because they'd made love? It could happen to a man, too, and it had happened to him tonight. He felt raw, exposed. His heart stung the way a sailor's eyes stung in salt spray, and he didn't know what to do.

What next?

He'd apologized to a lot of women in his time, for a lot of things.

Sorry I can't make our date tomorrow. Sorry I never called you back. Sorry I have to leave town so soon.

Mostly, those apologies had been accepted in the blink of an eye. Even when they hadn't been, it hadn't mattered; it had only served as proof of what he'd already known—that there was nothing of substance to the relationship in the first place.

This time, it was different.

This time, he didn't want the apology to be the final transaction, but Marisol hadn't given him a choice.

So, what next?

Right now he was too angry and too frustrated to
know, and he went on swimming his feelings away
for a long time.

The beige Ford Taurus pulled into the rental car lot
at Miami International Airport in plenty of time for a
9:00 a.m. flight to Washington, D.C., on Wednesday
morning. Two men sat in front, the younger at the
wheel and the elder, restless, in the passenger seat.

"If it was remotely safe, I'd stay another day," the
elder man said. "Nothing is cemented in place the
way I'd like."

"There was nothing we could do about it."

"DeBruzkya won't see it that way. I want a key
position in the Rebelian government, and to get that,
I need the leverage of success in this mission."

"I could stay on. Maybe there's some other way
we can—"

"No. Keep it simple. Don't change it at this late
stage. It's going to work this time, my gut is telling
me. My focus now has to be on the briefing in Washington. The information I get from that could be crucial to setting up Saturday's exercise correctly. The
U.S. Navy wants this sub almost as much as De-
Bruzkya does, but they'll put Evans Yachts and its
key players through a lot more hoops first."

"What do you hope to find out at the briefing?
Who's going to be there?"

"Gideon Faulkner will be there, and under a mi-
croscope."

"From what I've heard about the man, he'll handle
it like a kindergarten field trip."

"As to what I'll find out, I won't know until the

briefing takes place. Which is why I have to focus,
and let nothing slip. Friday night I'll be back here, in
uniform, with the other officers. We're dining chez
Evans, according to our program. That should be interesting."

"Don't drink too much," the younger man muttered under his breath, head turned toward the driver's
side window.

"I'm sorry?"

"Nothing. I'm wondering... Okay, someone's coming over with a clipboard. Looks like we can return
the car right here without going into the office."

"Excellent. We'll have time for a good breakfast
before the flight."

Marisol knew the best entrance to the hospital visitors' parking lot by this, her third drive up from Emerald Cove, but she was tired after a terrible night's
sleep and almost overshot the turn.

A car honked its horn repeatedly behind her, and
she yelled loudly, "Yes, I know! I'm sorry, okay?
You've made your point. Creep!" She knew that with
windows up and air-conditioning blasting in both vehicles, the other driver wouldn't hear.

She found Diego awake and sitting up in bed, reading a Spanish-language newspaper. He looked alert
enough to recognize her own level of fatigue and
stress, and she hoped he wouldn't. She didn't want
probing questions.

She'd prowled the garden paths for almost two
hours last night after reaching home, and even then
she'd slept restlessly, before getting up at six to drive
here. She'd felt Holt's hands on her body in her

dreams, reminding her of just how tangled her feelings toward him had become.

"You shouldn't have come," Diego said as soon as he saw her.

"Good to see you, too," she retorted.

"Of course it's good to see you." His voice softened. "But you look tired. You had to get up too early to do this. When are you supposed to be on the water?"

She shrugged. "Ten. I'll get back."

"And when will you eat?"

"In the car. Or on the boat."

Diego didn't say anything. He just reached for the phone beside his bed, and keyed in several numbers. "One extra large, with anchovy and black olive," he told the voice at the other end of the line.

"Oh, you! For breakfast?"

"How long will it take?" Diego asked, still on the phone. "Good." He gave his room number and a couple of directions, then cast a satisfied glare in Marisol's direction.

She shrugged helplessly. "I'm not going to argue."

"You see?"

"I was planning to eat."

"So it's just sleep you're trying to do without?"

"You're worse than Papa!"

"What's on your mind, *querida?*"

"You're much worse!"

"So I'll wait. I'm patient. Why come here, if you don't want to talk? You know I want you to save your energy."

A nurse came in—the same pretty, full-figured woman Diego had used his Spanish charm on two days ago. "Which hypocrite do I hear talking about saving energy?" she said.

Diego grinned. "Any suggestions for what I could do with my energy if I did save it, Caroline?" Now he called Nurse Meiklejohn by her first name, Marisol noted, and he spoke it as if he was rolling a fine wine in his mouth. "What's in it for me?"

"You don't need suggestions," she answered. "You have more than enough ideas of your own."

"I can tell you a few of them, if you like."

"Hmm." Nurse Caroline schooled her face carefully, but Marisol could see that she was seriously tempted and finding the situation difficult. She wasn't supposed to get personally involved with patients, just as yacht racers shouldn't get personally involved with their competitors.

The churning emotion in Marisol's gut heaved to the surface, and as soon as the nurse had done her work and left the room, she said, "Okay, Diego, you're right. I need to talk. I've got some questions, and I really need you to answer them straight." Her voice wobbled. "I think that you're the only person in my life right now whom I might actually be able to trust to do that!"

"Hmm," Diego said, just as Nurse Caroline had. He narrowed his eyes.

"When you suggested to Papa that I should lead the team, was it only because—" She stopped and tried again, her word choices more cautious. "In hindsight, do you think your personal feelings got in the way of your professional judgment, Diego?"

"I suspect that's what your father thinks," he answered.

"Oh, you know?"

"Yes, I know that." He smiled. "But he's wrong. Let me tell you about how I came to care for you so much, Marisol. About *why* I came to care, because that's more important. You've never met Rosaria, have you?"

Recognizing the name of Diego's ex-wife, Marisol shook her head. "No, I haven't."

"She hates the water. We had so little in common once that first frenzy of attraction ebbed away. She wouldn't even pretend an interest, wouldn't listen or learn, refused to try to understand why sailing was important to me. And of course I was at fault, too. We could have met each other halfway. That's so crucial in making a marriage last—meeting each other halfway."

"Is it?" Marisol murmured. "I suppose it is."

"As you and I got to know each other well, as you matured into such a fine woman and such a brilliant sailor, I started to think that for you and me to meet each other halfway would be so easy. So very easy. We had such a strong foundation of common interests, a shared understanding of priorities. No need ever to explain about sailing. It was such an attractive idea after the dreary end to my marriage, and I knew how much your father wanted it."

"He was wrong to make that so obvious."

"Maybe. It's not important. But sailing was where the whole thing started. Sailing came first, and it still does. No matter how much I felt for you, I never would have suggested you for the team leadership if I hadn't thought you could do it. That would have been cruel, to push you into a position I knew you couldn't fill. I have confidence in you, Marisol. You'll do better for the Villoria boats than Renaldo could have done.''

''Thank you.''

''Have I convinced you?''

''Of your faith in me, yes. That you're right to have it? I'm stubborn. I need proof. And I'm the only one who can give myself that.''

''You will.''

''I'll do my best.''

''You won yesterday.''

''So the trophy says. Some victories are worth more than others.''

''This one was worth a lot, wasn't it? Or is there something I don't know?''

She hesitated, then answered, ''Let's just go with what the trophy says, Diego. I'm very happy with the way I sailed yesterday.''

''So is your father.''

''Yes. It's good to hear Papa's praise.''

''You don't get to hear it enough.''

''That seems to be the general opinion. Lately I've started to value his holding back a little more because when I do get some approval from him at least I know he really means it.''

''I'm going to head off,'' Seth said in Holt's ear on Friday afternoon.

They stood with friends, family and strangers, leaning on the painted wooden guardrail that faced the ocean at Picnic Point Park as they watched the J-24-class race unfold on the triangular course set just within the wide arc of the bay.

The sun shone hot and strong, winning against a breeze that was much lighter here on shore than it was on the water. The air smelled of sunscreen and salt, and the palm trees behind them offered patches of thin shade.

"Before the end of the race?" Holt said.

"I really have to."

"Oh, the navy guys?"

"The navy guys," Seth confirmed, in a bare murmur. "Timetable I got from an aide at the Pentagon says their chopper is due to touch down at seventeen hundred thirty-five hours, and since this is the navy we're talking about…"

"Right. The chopper will touch down exactly on time, barring a global state of emergency."

"Which is about the level my adrenaline's at. I feel like a schoolboy about to show my big science project. Have we done the right thing, going ahead with this weekend when we know we could have a spy under our roof?"

"Was it your choice?"

"You're right. It wasn't. We were told to go ahead, try and bring the guy out into the open, if he is working from inside the system. But I could have argued more strongly against the idea and said our security wasn't good enough to take the risk."

"Yeah, the navy likes to hear that, when it's already handed over some pretty sensitive material to one of its contractors."

"Sometimes you're smarter than you look, little brother."

"And I look good, too."

"Head's a bit of a problem, though. Too big."

Holt managed to grin, but the grin faded as soon as Seth had threaded his way through the race-watching picnickers on their blankets, and had disappeared from sight.

Holt knew he didn't have nearly as big a head as some people thought, and even if he had, it would have shrunk by about fifty percent since Tuesday night.

He'd decided to give Marisol some space. He wanted her to realize how much he respected her and how clearly he understood that she wouldn't respond to being bulldozed or harassed or even charmed—especially not charmed—into accepting a second apology.

He wasn't even going to attempt such a thing.

Not yet, anyhow.

They'd seen each other several times since Tuesday night. During practices on the water. During yesterday's races, which they'd both been involved in. In the Clipper Bar, along with the Evans and Villoria crews from some of the smaller regatta events, unwinding afterward.

He'd smiled at her, waved, said hello, asked how she was. Formula phrase from him, formula reply from her. Hadn't gone any deeper than that. They couldn't have scraped together enough words from these brief exchanges to form even a quarter of a proper conversation. She'd signaled pretty clearly that she'd freeze him off if he got any closer.

It all added up to precisely nothing, in other words. So why did he feel as if he was in deeper than ever, with the way he felt about her?

Somehow, aware of her every move, he'd gotten to

know her better over the past three days. He'd seen
how she related to her crew in the bar. How available
she was, always ready to hear their gripes or their
ideas or their questions. He'd seen how hard she
worked on the boats. She was always the last to leave,
and always the first to step aboard after a race or a
practice she hadn't been involved in, to help stow the
gear or to debrief.

He'd seen how generous she was with journalists
and fans, too, even when some of them weren't particularly polite or respectful of her boundaries. She
had so much to give, and she was so generous in giving it.

She'd given him her body on Tuesday night, with
an open sensuality that he somehow understood had
been new to her, even though her vibrant, naked response suited her strength and her passion for life so
well.

He guessed that she couldn't be all that experienced. Fernando and his mother-in-law—Marisol's
beloved grandmother—would both have been protective of her, and Holt had the impression that she'd
been protective of herself in that area, too. She
wouldn't have slept with just anyone who asked,
wouldn't have given in to her body's fiery appetite
unless at some level her heart had also been involved.

So how long before she'd let her heart win? He
wondered.

They didn't have forever. They had sixty-some
hours, many of which would be taken up with tomorrow's big race. She would fly home to Spain on Monday morning, and they'd now wasted two and a half

precious days—half their potential time together—in barely speaking to each other.

It made him angry, and it made him scared.

Maybe I'm wrong, he thought. Maybe I'm the only one who feels this could go somewhere. Maybe it's that old instinct to win coming to the surface, the instinct that she dislikes and distrusts in me—which isn't fair, because she has it as strongly as I do. Do I only want her because she's proving impossible to get? Because she's the big winner's trophy? The brass ring? Couldn't be that, could it? Am I that shallow? That out of touch with who I really am? Damn her, she won't let me find out!

"I don't think you're going to win this one, Holt!" said a perky voice just to his left.

Holt blinked. Either he'd been speaking out loud or his petite blond cousin, Honey Evans Strong, had been reading his mind. He didn't like either possibility, until he realized she was talking about the yacht race. Honey, her husband Maxwell and their two-week-old baby boy had taken a leisurely drive down from their home in Maryland this week to enjoy the spectacle of the yachts parading the bay.

Holt focused on the water for the first time in ten minutes, and picked out the sail number and turquoise spinnaker of the Evans boat. It wasn't in the lead. The orange-and-royal-blue spinnaker ballooning out in front of the leading boat belonged to the British *Time and Tide*.

"I guess we're not," he answered his cousin.

"You don't seem all that crushed by the imminent prospect of defeat." With her curly hair, blue eyes and shapely figure, Honey looked like a princess doll, but she had a smart mind and took pride in using it.

"I don't have a lot invested in this race on a personal level," Holt answered.

"You're saving your investment for *Unicorn*'s performance tomorrow, right?"

"Yeah, even there, though, I..." He trailed off on a sigh.

Honey looked astonished.

"Okay, this is the point where you need to put your hand under your chin and pull up the face mask, you impostor," she teased. "The real Holt Evans might pretend he's more interested in chasing women than chasing winds, but he'd never just stand there with his shoulders all drooped and sound as if he simply couldn't be bothered. What's up, cuz?"

"You're right." He spread his hands, tried to sound careless and amused. "I admit it. I'd rather be chasing women than chasing winds."

"No, I said you *pretend* that. I can see through you like glass, Holt. Something's getting to you."

"Women are getting to me. You included."

She looked at him in silence for a moment, then seemed to accept that he was serious. She put on a smile. "Okay, I'll stop teasing, if you tell me my baby's gorgeous." Little Max was fast asleep in a soft fabric sling across his mother's front.

"He's gorgeous. He's adorable. Can I buy him?"

"No, but I can give you the instructions on how to make your own."

"I got those in grade school."

"Yeah, but it's more complex than people think. There are secret ingredients no one tells you about."

"Too deep for me right now, Honey."

At this, she just clicked her tongue and shook her head and he felt like shouting, Don't have this conversation with me! Have it with that beautiful woman standing over there, about twenty yards away, with the long black hair flipping in the breeze and the pretty little top hugging her breasts, and the backside so cute I could eat it for breakfast. *She's* the one with the problem!

Time and Tide won the race.

Holt tried to care, but couldn't.

In the overall standings, the Evans team was very slightly in the lead. Tomorrow there were a couple more minor races scheduled, following the triangular course around the buoys in the bay, while out to sea the maxi yachts and some of the other larger keelboats would engage in their far more dramatic struggle for victory on the blue water, heading for the finish line in the Bahamas, over a hundred nautical miles away.

"And I'm really, seriously, supposed to care about that," he muttered to himself. "I know I am."

The crowd along the park's sea-facing guardrail began to break up, now that the race was over. People went back to their picnic blankets or their cars or bicycles chained in the rack near the small pay parking lot.

There were plenty of other vantage points for viewing the yachts. This was one of the more relaxed locations, which was why Holt and Seth and the others had chosen it. No journalists, no party animals, yet it offered a good perspective on the trickiest side of the triangular course. Maybe this was why Marisol and a few of the Villoria crew were also here.

Holt watched her covertly, leaning his elbow on the knobby trunk of a king palm. She was speaking to Renaldo Tejerizo in rapid Spanish, her hands making lines and shapes in the air. He didn't have to speak the language to know she was talking about the race.

He made hand movements like that himself when he talked about sailing. Not as graceful, not as beautiful or as bold. But they meant the same thing. One hand was the boat, and the other was the wind. The Villoria J-24 had powered home in third place, just seconds behind the two boats in front. She must be talking about what the crew could have done to better that result.

Tejerizo nodded, evidently agreeing with her. Seconds later, he looked out to sea, looked at his watch, looked at what the breeze was doing in the tops of the palms, and caught sight of Holt. He raised his hand in a casual salute, which Holt returned. Marisol had seen him now, also.

Okay, this was the moment. This was the way to make himself care about tomorrow's race again, as he needed to. Clear the thick air between himself and Marisol. Give it a final shot.

He levered himself fully upright with a nudge of his elbow and walked toward the pair. "Could I have a minute, Marisol?"

She nodded, one neat, tiny jerk of her chin. "Of course." She added something to Renaldo in Spanish, and he said good-bye to both of them and left, heading along the curving beachfront promenade. The Villoria crew's hotel wasn't far from here.

As soon as he'd gone, Marisol's whole face

changed and tightened. She looked defensive, hostile, ready to go on the attack. Holt got in first.

"This is crazy," he said. "I can already see you're about to bite my head off."

"Not at all. Why would I risk breaking my teeth?"

"I messed up on Tuesday, okay? I know that. With what I did, and the way I told you about it. I've apologized, and I'll apologize again. I was wrong to give you even a second's leeway in that race. But you have to accept that I didn't do it for bad reasons. I did it for the best reason in the world. We should give this a second chance, Marisol."

"I have more important things to think about right now."

"No, you don't! The race tomorrow? I'm trying to care about it, but I can't, because this matters more."

"This?"

"Us! Giving ourselves a chance."

He took hold of her shoulders and ran his hands down her upper arms. She didn't twist away, but she straightened her back and lifted her chin and glared at him. The sides of her breasts nudged his thumbs, and he wanted to slide his fingers across and explore their weight, wrap his arms around her and hold her. Her mouth, with the tiny, uneven dent in its upper lip was soft and still, glistening with moisturizing lip balm— made to be kissed.

He bent toward her, enveloped in the scent of her sunscreen. She smelled like a day on the water, salty and hot and fresh. It was a familiar smell that he loved. "We were electric together on Tuesday night," he said, watching that mouth and remembering with every nerve ending in his body.

''Is that supposed to make up for what you did?''
Her voice came out too low and unsteady, which gave
him a little hope. She might try to pretend that she
couldn't feel the electricity, but her entire vibrant body
said she was lying. ''The humiliation that I can't even
tell anyone about?'' she continued. ''I have to pretend
to be proud of a win that wasn't really mine! Pretend
to Papa, Diego, my brothers, Renaldo, the press, the
crew. Do you know how hard that is to live with?''

''It was a mistake,'' he answered, still watching her
mouth and her eyes, wanting her, wanting to kiss her
anger into oblivion. ''I've said that. And I have to live
with it, too. Live with the fear that one bad impulse
out on the water is going to ruin the promise of the
best night of my life.''

She looked startled at this. Her eyes widened, her
lips parted, her tongue lapped nervously against her
teeth then disappeared again. But he soon saw that he
still hadn't gotten through to her.

''How many of those have you had, I wonder?''
she said, her black eyes glittering behind narrowed
lids and a forest of lashes.

''One, Marisol,'' he said. ''I've had one best night.
With you. I'm asking if there could be more. With
you,'' he repeated heavily, just in case she hadn't gotten the point. ''But it's obvious the answer's no, and
I don't hang around where I'm not wanted, so I guess
this is it. Good luck for tomorrow.''

He let go of her soft arms, stepped back and stuck
his hand out, daring her.

You don't want us to be lovers, Marisol? Fine.
We'll be competitors. Competitors shake hands. Let's
see how you deal with that.

She took the dare, apparently understanding his thought process without him putting it into words. Their palms and fingers slid across each other. Her hand had been cooled and dried by the breeze from the water. Her skin wasn't as soft and supple as he remembered it from Tuesday night. She'd been working hard. Neglecting her skin-care routine. She might pretend otherwise, but she was falling apart just the way he was.

He shook her hand slowly, then let her go, holding their eye contact, willing her into a betrayal of what she felt beneath the facade. And he got it. Was almost sure that he'd gotten it, anyhow. A flicker and a falter in her gaze. She looked down, looked up again, smiled a smile that stopped before it even got halfway up her face.

Yes, she'd pushed him away, but it hadn't been easy for her.

"Good luck to the *Unicorn,* too, Holt," she said. "We'll meet up in Nassau, when the race is over."

"Yeah, we will."

Right now, he couldn't think that far ahead. He felt like a medieval sailor who believed that the earth was flat and that he'd almost reached the edge. Sometime tomorrow, the current was going to get hold of him and he'd go spilling over the side. What lay beyond, he had no idea.

Eleven

None of the three computer weather models that Holt consulted could agree on what lay in store for the next day. Evans Yachts had a professional meteorologist under contract to provide them with his interpretations of the data, also. He and Holt met at Evans Yachts' headquarters at five o'clock on Friday afternoon, and the two of them achieved a better consensus than the computers did.

They agreed that the weather picture for tomorrow looked confusing.

"I've said this before, Holt," Rod Nagle told him. "It's not an exact science."

"So remind me, why does Evans Yachts pay you to do this for us?"

"Because it's an art. It's instinct. It's fortune telling. And my crystal ball is pretty good."

"Okay, so get it out and tell me what you see when the mist clears."

"When the mist clears, I see more mist. Clouds. Wind. Rain. There are going to be storms."

"Only one of the computer models agrees with you."

"Two of them agree, but one of those two puts the storm area out of race range. I think that one's wrong."

"Can we look at the printouts again?"

"Sure." Rod spread out numerous maps and charts and sheets of data on the big table in the Evans Yachts executive conference room where Holt had virtually held him prisoner for the past twenty minutes.

"How many other crews are using you for their forecasts?"

"A couple," Rod answered. The information as to who paid for his services was considered confidential. Accurate interpretation of weather data could give a crew a critical edge. "And a couple more are using a different service. The rest are relying on the bulletins that the regatta organizers are issuing."

"Which computer model do they work from?"

"The one that puts the storms off the map, to the south."

"What kind of storms are we talking about here?"

"Localized, pushing changeable winds ahead of them. Not the kind that gets named like a baby and makes the network news. The kind where one place can get an inch of rain in half an hour, while a few miles away they're basking in sunshine. That is, unless we go with the model that says this low pressure area could expand, in which case—"

"Not to interrupt or anything, Rod," Holt said, suddenly weary of the whole thing. "But I think I'm ready for the bottom line."

"Bottom line? Be prepared. You and your crew are solely responsible for the decision to race—"

"—according to the international rules of sailing. I know. Barring an actual hurricane, though, we'll be out there. I'm more concerned about what sails we'll need, whether we'll get to run with the spinnaker for most of the race, whether there's a chance we can run ahead of the storm winds and use them to our advantage."

"I'll say it again. Be prepared. Check your life rafts and your flares and your E.P.I.R.B." Like any sailor, Holt recognized the abbreviation. It stood for Emergency Position Indicator Radio Beacon. "Pack those extra storm sails."

"They add weight."

"They save lives. It's not always the safest course of action to run on bare poles in storm conditions. I'm a sailor too, remember."

"Crazy, like the rest of us, in other words."

"Yep."

"Thanks, Rod. I know you've done your best on this. One thing I didn't want for tomorrow, though, was an ambiguous forecast."

As he said it, Holt heard a second meaning to his words. At least Marisol hadn't given him an ambiguous forecast an hour ago after the J-24 race. She'd been painfully clear on the fact that there was no future for the two of them, however much her body might be urging her to give a different answer.

Would they have gotten to this point sooner or later in any case, even if they hadn't made love, and even if he hadn't thrown Tuesday's race? Chemistry could work both ways. Maybe the mix between them was always going to be far too volatile. His actions in the Laser-class solo simply provided a convenient excuse for her to bail out.

Holt walked Rod out to the elevator, then went back and prowled through the offices for a while. The Evans team of boat designers had gone for the day, and so had the rest of headquarters staff. Across town, the boat-building yard itself would be quiet now, too, its sheds and equipment locked up, guarded and fully alarmed. Arriving back in the conference room, he glanced at the clock on the wall.

Five thirty-four.

He heard the air beating in the distance outside, and went to the window in time to see the dark shape of a helicopter skimming across the sea. It headed toward the helipad next to one of the boat canals that stretched its long wet finger back from the bay, and settled to the ground like a clumsy dragonfly.

The navy was right on time.

Seth had already told him not to front up for the dinner with the naval officers tonight. "Keep your head clear for tomorrow. This sub isn't the only piece of marine technology we care about around here. Focus on *Unicorn* and on your race."

"Yeah, thanks, I'll do that," he'd promised.

Now might be a good time to put that promise into action.

He gathered up the sheafs of maps and weather data and slid them into a waterproof plastic pouch. He'd head down to the marina, pick up a pizza and a beer on the way, and eat dinner alone on the boat. The quiet and the solitude would clear his head, help him to focus on strategy and planning.

He'd do as Rod had suggested, too, and check the emergency equipment, maybe compromise a little on weight and add a couple of spare items, like a particular storm sail.

He'd have the pizza and the beer first, however.

Or maybe two pizzas, and two beers.

He didn't get to *Unicorn* until after six, by which
time hunger had clawed right to the top of his stomach. He ate on deck, hunkered down beside the wheel
and largely shielded from the view of sightseers on
the marina's public docks. The western sky turned on
a trademark Florida Keys sunset, in swathes of orange
and pink and mauve. The pizza filled his growling gut,
and the beer foamed in his mouth, as cold as Atlantic
storm spray.

It got dark and quiet, and a sense of peace settled
over him. Light from the buildings that fronted the
bay spilled out across the silky, midnight-blue water.
He could hear music and laughter and conversation
coming from patios and boat decks. The air was warm,
too humid for some people, but he was used to it. He
didn't think about anything very much, kept his mind
deliberately empty and just enjoyed the sense of being
alone.

Not quite alone.

Most of the boats in this section of the marina were
dark, closed up and alarmed, but there were a couple
of crews at work, making last-minute checks or repairs
or adjustments to their equipment. Holt remembered
that he'd wanted to do the same.

He went below deck and got out the emergency
equipment, checked for rust, water damage, missing
parts or flat batteries, and ran through various sets of
instructions for use. You didn't really want to have a
lot of practical, in-the-field experience in activating
E.P.I.R.B.s, setting off flares or inflating life rafts.

He checked the weather fax, which would give
them meteorological updates during the race, and
again on Sunday when they had to sail back from

Nassau to Emerald Cove. He looked at the sails bun-
dled below deck and queried one of his earlier
choices. He'd talk to his most experienced crew members tomorrow morning, when maybe the forecast
would be clearer, and get some more opinions.

Back on deck, he saw that there was a light in *Skyrider*'s cabin. Crew at work on last minute details,
there, too? He couldn't see any sign of activity. Then
a figure appeared from below, and he realized after
just a few seconds that it was Marisol. He knew the
way she moved now, recognized her silhouette and
the way she knotted her hair securely on top of her
head when she was on the boat.

He had no good reason to keep watching her, but
he did. Even got out the binoculars he kept below
deck, because he couldn't see enough of what she was
doing from this distance.

Okay, now he could see.

She was preparing to take a swim. She looked
around to make sure she was alone, hung a towel on
the rail, pulled off her skirt and tank top, unfastened
her bra and dropped it on top of the other clothing on
the deck.

Then she dove from the bow, making a light, almost
phosphorescent splash of white as she hit the water.
He lowered the binoculars and followed her progress
through the water by the wake she left behind her—a
different pattern in the dancing of the angular snippets
of light on the dark surface, which soon settled into
near-stillness once more.

She struck directly out into the bay, swimming
strong and straight, with curved arms, a neat kick and
bilateral breathing on every third stroke. He lost this

detail when she went too far out, and he was just starting to get nervous for her—what about sharks, power boats and unexpected currents?—when she turned and powered back in.

Beside *Skyrider* she rested in the water, floating on her back with her arms stretched out. Holt raised the binoculars again, wondering if he could possibly catch her expression. Or maybe she'd look in this direction, and he'd know she was still thinking about him, the way he couldn't stop thinking about her.

As he watched, she tucked her body out of the back float and reached the side of the boat in a couple of strokes. She climbed the rope ladder that hung down from the deck and he got a clear view.

Black hair still piled on top of her head. Strong, neat shoulders. Spine streaming with the water spilling from all that beautiful hair. Thong-backed panties.

She leaned to grab her towel, then swung it up to dry her hair, facing out to the water as she toweled the dripping black mass. Her breasts bounced and her nipples were pebbled from the chill of the breeze on her wet skin.

Holt lowered the binoculars again, disgusted with himself. This was nothing better than voyeurism. If she'd seen him, especially with the binoculars, she never would have swum at all. And since when did he need to spy on a half-naked woman to get his thrills?

He went below deck, put the binoculars away and made himself a mug of instant coffee, sugary and black. He didn't want to draw attention to his presence at this point by closing up and leaving the boat. He'd wait until the coast was clear.

* * *

Marisol saw the light in *Unicorn*'s cabin as she picked up her pile of clothing to go get dressed again below deck. She didn't know who was on the boat. It could have been anyone from the Evans crew. No reason to think it was Holt.

The swim had been great. Always a little scary to be out in the middle of a bay and out of her depth after dark, but she made a point of taking swims like this occasionally. One day she might be in a situation where the waters of Emerald Cove would seem like a child's wading pool by comparison, and she wanted to take what precautions she could to eliminate the element of panic.

Panic was bad.

Panic exhausted you, slashed the length of time you could survive in the water, robbed you of vital air if you were trapped beneath an upturned hull, and took away your ability to think rationally about how to stay alive. If she ever went overboard or holed her boat, panic must not enter into the equation.

The swim had invigorated her, too. Her freshly cooled skin tingled and her mind felt alert. She had a couple of last-minute checks to make on the equipment, and she wanted to think about that ambiguous forecast a little more, also. She'd noticed a couple of the other boats bringing new sails on board earlier, when she'd arrived at the marina after eating in the Clipper Bar with Violetta and Xavier.

With the latest weather fax sitting in front of her—and, to be honest, not making a lot of sense—she drank a glass of water and thought about heading home. Had the swim relaxed her enough to give her a good night's sleep? Was there anything else she needed to take care of tonight?

She heard a noise outside, and at first thought it was coming from the boat moored adjacent to *Skyrider*. Then she felt the slight but unmistakable dip and heave of the hull as someone stepped on board. Who was it? The light was on here in the cabin. Surely it must be obvious that she was here, but no one had called out.

The boat still rocked faintly, but there was no further sound. She listened, holding her breath, and then, after what felt like nearly a minute, she heard footsteps. Rather than waiting for whoever it was to come to her, she took the initiative and climbed up on deck.

"Renaldo." They came face to face as soon as she stepped from the cabin.

"I was looking for you," he said.

"Very quietly."

"I wasn't sure if I really wanted to find you."

"Gee, that's a bit complicated," she mocked, her voice light.

And it was out of character, she thought. Renaldo Tejerizo wasn't a complicated man.

"Can we close up the boat for tonight, find a place where I might get a decent espresso?" he suggested.

Madre de Dios, he wanted to talk!

"Sure," she said, hiding her surprise.

They stowed the gear she'd checked and set the alarms, talking a little about tomorrow as they worked. Leaving the marina, Marisol looked across at *Unicorn* and saw that whoever had been there earlier must have left. Holt's boat was as dark and silent as *Skyrider*.

"The Clipper Bar?" Renaldo suggested.

"How's their coffee?"

"No one in America knows how to make good coffee, so it'll be no worse and no better than anywhere else."

"You said you wanted a decent espresso. Papa prides himself on his coffee. Do you want—"

"I don't want to talk about this with your father," Renaldo answered quickly.

She thought not. She'd only used the issue of good coffee to test her intuition.

"In that case," she said, "the Clipper Bar is fine."

The place was still crowded. Marisol would have liked to sit outside, but Renaldo skulked at once to the darkest corner he could find, where the only breeze would come from the flap of the nearby swing door that led through to the bathrooms. She waited while he went up to the bar and ordered decaf for her and an espresso for himself.

Sitting opposite her, he said, "Who would win tomorrow, Marisol, if both *Unicorn* and *Skyrider* were knocked out of the race?"

Were they here to talk about race strategy? She hadn't gotten that impression when he'd first turned up on the boat. Hiding her surprise once again, she gave him the best answer she could, while he poured an avalanche of sugar into the puddle of black liquid in his cup.

"Possibly the same boat that would win if *Unicorn* and *Skyrider* weren't knocked out of the race, Renaldo," she said. "All of the maxis are so strong. There are seven maxis racing, and I'd give five of them a chance at line honors. People talk about Villoria and Evans as the main rivals, and that's flattering, but the *British Blue* and *Lavazzi* and *Omega* teams are all very competitive, and the boats are impressive.''

''So why would someone from one of those teams approach me with some tale about wanting—'' He shook his head. ''It doesn't make sense! He wanted me to sabotage the Evans boat.''

''What?''

''He said the blame would fall on your father. He got that right, I guess. There is a rivalry between the two companies, although a reasonably friendly one. But even if that did knock out both Evans and Villoria, there are, as you say, three other boats with an equal chance. He said if I did what he wanted, there'd be a captaincy for me on his team's winning boat, as well as a cash payment, but he can't know that his boat will win. I've been thinking about it. I guess he hoped the money would blind me, and I wouldn't think it through, but his story doesn't make sense. I don't think he was connected with another racing team at all.''

Marisol had a fistful of questions, but she began with just one. ''Did you take the money?''

He took a noisy sip of his black brew. ''I was going to,'' he answered.

Silence.

Marisol waited, knowing there was more to come.

''I was pretty angry, earlier in the week,'' he went on. ''You know why. I was passed over.''

''And if you'd gotten the captaincy, I would have been passed over. We both deserved it, Renaldo. Only one of us could have it.''

''You've held the team together and gotten better results than I'd feared,'' Renaldo agreed grudgingly.

He drew in a mouthful of sweet coffee between his teeth. "I'm still not happy, but..." He gave a Mediterranean shrug.

"So what held you back?"

"Number one, I didn't see what I had to get out of it. Other than money. But if I was interested in money, I wouldn't be crazy enough to choose sailing as a profession, so there you go. Number two, what I told you just now. I don't believe this guy has ties to any of the other teams, which means his whole story was a lie. And I don't do anything when I'm not told the truth about why I'm doing it."

"If you turned the man down, then you didn't have to tell me about any of this."

"You want Holt Evans's boat out of the race?"

"No! But—"

"Marisol, someone else is going to blow up that boat during tomorrow's race."

"That's impossible." Realizing how much her voice had risen, she lowered it. They'd spoken in Spanish the whole time, but Florida was full of people who were fluent in the language. "Security is tight here," she said. "The boats are alarmed. Who could get access? Surely that's why this stranger approached you in the first place. He needed someone with a security pass to the guarded end of the marina, and a knowledge of how boat alarm systems operate. You turned him down, so nothing's going to happen."

"He had someone else." Renaldo shook his head, drained his coffee to the dregs. "He tried to leverage my agreement by talking about this other guy, when I told him the answer was no." Renaldo quoted in a theatrical voice, "'If you can't recognize an opportunity when it falls in your lap, we have someone else who can, someone whose access to the Evans boat will be even easier than yours.'''

"So why did the man approach you at all if he had someone else?"

"I don't know."

"There was another Evans boat destroyed a few months ago—a catamaran the family used for private sailing. Holt told me about it. He said it was an engine explosion. An accident. But now I'm wondering…"

"Yes, seems like too much of a coincidence," Renaldo agreed. "They do some pretty secret designing and building at Evans Yachts. They've had U.S. Navy contracts in the past. Maybe this isn't about racing at all."

"I need to tell Holt. Tonight. He'll be at home. I'll get a cab."

"What makes you think he'll be at home?"

"We have a big race tomorrow, and it's nearly ten."

"He has a reputation for staying out late, race or no race."

"I can get his cell phone number from his mother."

"And he's not usually alone."

Marisol flushed. "Are you saying I shouldn't interrupt his date?"

Renaldo looked at her, mouth tucked in at one corner, a single eyebrow raised. "Your father won't like it if you get hurt."

"I'm not in the market for getting hurt by Holt Evans, Renaldo."

She wasn't in the market, because he'd already hurt her.

Or she'd hurt herself.

When you did something stupid on a boat and got injured in consequence, who did you blame? Yourself or the boat? She'd done something very stupid with Holt on Tuesday night.

Twice.

And she'd gotten hurt.

But three days later, she was angrier with herself than with him. She couldn't let it get in the way. The possibility of sabotage to his boat had to override all other considerations.

"You won't get hurt, even if he's in bed with a woman when he picks up his phone?" Renaldo said.

"No. Not even if he's in bed with three!"

Renaldo clicked his tongue and grinned, as if he thought Holt might be on to a good thing, in that case.

Marisol's face burned even hotter, and she was thankful for the murky lighting in the bar. "Whom he's sleeping with is not my concern. You did the right thing to tell me all this. If you're not aware of the fact, I value your contribution to the team."

"Save it," he growled. "Let's go."

Marisol nodded and stood, flung a couple of bills on the table and left the bar, chased by the vivid image of Holt getting rid of his pre-race tension with one— or more—of the willing Florida blondes who'd flocked around him for as long as she could remember.

Holt wasn't at home.

Marisol spoke with his father, Russ, who gave her the unsurprising information that he didn't keep all that close a track on his adult son's movements. He did come up with a cell phone number, but didn't invite Marisol to use one of the phones in the house to make her call. From behind him, she heard the rumble of male voices and the sound of silverware on china plates. The palatial home was all lit up. They had company tonight.

"There isn't a problem, is there?" In his sixties, like her own father, Russ Evans was still a very impressive man, with Holt's blue eyes set in a shrewd and confident face.

"Just a question about the race," she hedged, already stepping back off the wide front porch. If she was about to send any member of the Evans family off on a wild goose chase in quest of nonexistent saboteurs, she'd prefer it to be Holt, not his dad.

"If you'll excuse me, then," Holt's father said.

"Yes. You have guests. I'm sorry to interrupt. If Holt has his cell phone turned off and I can't track him down…"

"I'll make sure he gets a message."

"Thanks." Once out beyond the high gates that opened onto the main driveway, she took out her own cell, keyed in the sequence of numbers Russ Evans had given her and got Holt right away.

"Marisol?" His voice sounded husky as he said her name, and she couldn't help wondering. Husky with lovemaking? Where was he right now?

Just this afternoon he'd asked her to forgive him for Tuesday's mistake and she'd turned him down. Had she done the right thing? He couldn't know how hard it had been for her to reject that perfectly performed apology of his. And that was exactly why she'd rejected it.

Because it was too perfect.

The best night of his life?

Oh, give me a break!

She was with Renaldo on this one. With his reputation, and the way she'd seen him operate with her own eyes, back in their teens, she found it a lot easier to believe he would have a naked woman beside him right now, five hours after the emotional plea he'd made to her, than to believe that the ''best night of his life'' stuff was genuine.

She wished he'd never said it, wished with all her heart that he'd sounded a lot less smooth and a lot more vulnerable, the way she felt herself where he was concerned.

''I—I hope I'm not interrupting anything.'' Leaning against one of the Evans mansion's big stone gateposts, in the lee of the night breeze and with her back to the street, she hunched her shoulders instinctively as she pressed the phone to her ear, getting ready to cradle the punch in the gut that she'd experience if she heard a woman's breathy giggle in the background.

''Such as?'' His voice dropped even lower, as if he didn't want to be overheard.

''Anything.'' She closed her eyes, willing her voice to remain steady and matter-of-fact. ''I'm calling from just outside your place, and I know you're not at home. Please excuse me if—''

''You're not interrupting anything, Marisol,'' he said right beside her as he laid a hand on her bare shoulder.

She almost jumped out of her skin.

* * *

"After I left the boat tonight I drove around for a while, then I saw you coming down the driveway as I was about to make the turn," Holt said. He gestured at his car, pulled over to the curb a little farther along.

Marisol had her hand pressed to her heart, and didn't look as if she'd started breathing again yet. He didn't apologize or attempt to soothe her shattered equilibrium, just grinned at her as he flipped his cell phone into his pocket, enjoying the fact that he'd made her feel *something,* even if it was only shock.

"And instead I pictured you— I thought you might have been with— I didn't want to trespass on—"

For a couple of seconds he didn't understand her awkwardness and her inability to get to the end of a sentence. Then it hit him. She'd thought she might have been interrupting a date. After what he'd said to her this afternoon? Man, her opinion of him was low!

He dammed his anger down in his gut, kept his voice cool as he observed, "Must be pretty important, then, for you to risk, uh… Let's just say for you to risk knocking me out of the game at second or third base. Or did you like the idea of spoiling my night?"

Yeah, he was lashing back at her. Because he was hurt. Not that she'd believe that.

If her opinion of him was so low, what did it say about her opinion of herself, after Tuesday night?

The question pulled him up short, set off a chain reaction of possibilities in his head that he didn't have time to explore right now. And it made him regret, already, the things he'd just said.

"Look," he added. "Forget any of that, okay? Please tell me why you're here."

He tried to take her hand, but she wouldn't let him anywhere near her. Her stiffly held body and the formality of her manner were as good as a force field, as good as the anti-sonar shield Gideon Faulkner had developed for the Stingray sub. She had her hands clasped tightly in front of her and her elbows pressed into her sides.

"Holt, there's something I have to tell you that could potentially be very important." She swallowed, didn't seem to know where to go next.

He tried to help her. "About tomorrow's race?"

In the back of his mind, he was still thinking about the way she'd pictured him at the far end of the phone. In bed with some other woman. This soon. With the way he'd been feeling since Tuesday—no, since Saturday—he couldn't imagine putting himself through the kind of hoops that women like Tori and Heather required before they let you take them to bed, ever again. And he couldn't imagine enjoying himself when he got there, even if he did.

"Connected to the race," Marisol answered. "Connected to your family's boatyard, and some of the work that's being done there. Possibly it's connected to what you told me the other night, about your brother's catamaran exploding. I have to ask. Was that really an accident, Holt?"

Now she had his attention, one hundred percent. "What did you hear? Who told you it wasn't?"

"So I'm right. It was sabotage."

"We didn't let that information go public. Evans Yachts is working on something for the navy. And it's not plumbing fixtures. I shouldn't even tell you that much."

"You don't have to tell me anything. But I need to tell you that one of our crew was approached earlier this week with the offer of a big payment if he rigged a bomb on *Unicorn,* timed to explode during tomorrow's race. Whoever it was pretended to represent a rival team, but the crewman realized that didn't make sense. He turned the offer down, thought about it and came to me. The man who approached him let slip that he has a backup candidate for the role, Holt. Someone with 'easy access' to the marina and to the boat."

"Someone in the crew?"

"Or someone who works for Evans Yachts. I wish I had more detail to give you, but I don't."

"Has to be someone who works for us. I don't see anyone on *Unicorn*'s racing crew who'd take on a suicide bombing, and anyhow most of them weren't around in June when Seth's boat went up."

"Then you're taking this seriously? I was right to tell you about it."

"Absolutely! We've tightened our security systems so much over the past few months." He spoke half to himself, thinking out loud. Marisol's big dark eyes fixed on his face. She didn't look so stiff and distant anymore. She was caught up in this, concerned.

Concerned for him.

"Then you're safe," she said. "No one could sabotage the boat. If there's even a chance that something could happen to you and your crew tomorrow, Holt…" She swallowed suddenly and her black eyes shone with moisture. "It's horrifying!"

"Unfortunately, the one place that's out of the loop with our new security is *Unicorn*. We've watched for competitors stealing our stuff, and we've kept our new hull finish under wraps, but the idea of the boat as an enemy target…'' He shook his head. ''These guys are right, though. Blow up the boat right in the middle of the race, split the focus of everyone involved. If they've already identified any kind of weak link in our arrangements for secrecy, they could get what they want.''

He dragged his keys from his pocket and turned back to his car.

''Where are you going?''

''To the boat. Do you mind coming along?''

''I— No, that's fine. If you think I'm of any use. Holt, I know things went badly between us.'' She paused. ''And it was my fault, too. Not just yours. I shouldn't have suggested that it was. This possibility of sabotage is the last thing you want to be dealing with right now. Of course I'll come with you.''

''If you can remember anything more about what your crewman said… Who was it?''

''Renaldo.''

''We saw him the other night,'' Holt said as they reached the car. ''He walked you home, remember?''

''Yes, and he was talking to someone. I didn't see the other man until I reached Renaldo, and then he disappeared into the Clipper Bar immediately.''

''So you wouldn't know him if you saw him again?''

''No. I really didn't see him at all.'' She frowned. ''I heard him, though.''

''You heard him speak?'' Holt started the engine, shot the car into gear and made a tight turn in the middle of the street.

"No. I heard him cough," Marisol said. "He sounded like one of those plastic squeeze toys with a squeaker that toddlers have, or a Pekinese dog with a chest cold. High pitched and wheezy, with almost a whistle in it."

"We should remember that."

They reached the marina in a few minutes and parked in a side street, out of sight of the waterfront. There were only two of the racing boats lit up by this time, and the security guard at the checkpoint looked bored. One of the lit boats was *Unicorn.* At first, as they approached, the elegant maxi appeared deserted, but then Holt saw a single figure slumped beside the wheel with his face buried in his hands, right where he himself had eaten his pizza and drunk his beer a few hours earlier.

The man looked up at the sound of Holt and Marisol's footsteps, and Holt recognized him right away.

"Is there a mechanical problem with the boat, Riley?" he asked quietly. "You should tell me about it, not deal with it on your own. And you know that."

Riley Walker, forty-seven-year-old husband and father of three, who'd worked on building Evans boats for almost fifteen years, hid his face in his hands again as his body began to shake with silent sobs.

Twelve

"You planted the bomb on Seth's boat," Holt yelled at the defeated man on the yacht. "You betrayed the people you've worked with for half of your working life. My decent, caring brother—*my brother*—who's given you time off whenever you needed it and loaned you money for your wife's medical bills. Seth and Emma were almost killed!"

He leaped onto the boat, grabbed Riley's shirt with both fists and dragged the man to his feet. Seeing his intention, Marisol was right behind him. "No, Holt!"

He didn't listen. "You attacked my cousin Drew's fiancée. How much were you paid to do that?" He had the fabric of Riley's T-shirt so tightly screwed up in one hand that the neck of the shirt had tightened across the man's throat and would soon choke him. His other fist balled and moved back, ready to strike. Riley made no attempt to defend himself. He looked as if he'd aged by ten years in just this one night.

Marisol lunged at Holt from behind, trapped his arms in the crooks of her elbows and tried to pull him back. They struggled with each other, muscle on muscle, and Marisol knew she couldn't win through force. Holt was too strong. Another second and he'd get his arms free and throw her off his back like an unwanted winter coat. "Why the hell shouldn't I do this?" he demanded through gritted teeth.

"Because you need to hear his story," she told him urgently. "You need facts, not revenge. If he's unconscious—"

"I want him unconscious. I want him in the hospital!"

"No, you don't. You want information."

Riley still stood as if frozen, his dry sobs subsiding and his head bowed. He was a puppet of a man, with broken strings.

"Okay. Okay." Holt stilled in her arms, and she felt his heavy breathing against her breasts, felt the rippling muscles in his back slowly unknot, felt his arms drop to his sides.

She didn't let go. Didn't yet trust Holt's intentions.

"He may know something about the man who hired him," she said. "Promise me you'll use your head on this, Holt."

"Seth won't thank me if I don't," he growled. "Okay, you're right, Marisol. Yes. Thank you. Walker, I want the full story."

All right. It was safe now. Marisol trailed her fingers across his back as she released him, filled with a treacherous longing to keep holding him, to rediscover the pleasure of having his body in her arms, to smell the sea-tanged scent of him. She shivered, stepped back and only now felt the way the boat was rocking after their struggle.

"I didn't want anyone to get hurt," Riley said. "And I never attacked Alison Myers. Maybe the attack was connected to the rest of this, but I had nothing to do with it. You have to believe me on that,

Holt. I messed up. A few months ago a guy said he'd been hired by another boatyard that needed a big contract Evans had tendered for, to save its business. They wanted to put Evans out of the running. He offered me money. He'd found out we had medical bills, and that it looked like we were going to lose the house. I turned him down, but then he started talking about Jeri."

"He threatened to hurt your wife?" Holt cut in.

"Said how she was home by herself some of the time, wasn't she? And hadn't I ever thought about what might happen if someone broke into our house and she couldn't run, couldn't get to the phone or call for help? How someone could easily rough her up, hurt her real bad, and she wouldn't even be able to describe who did it. She can't talk real good anymore, you see. The multiple sclerosis has gotten to her speech."

"Hell, Riley!"

"That was when I said okay, I'd do it."

"You didn't go to Seth or Dad?"

"I knew some of that stuff we were working on was secret. I thought Mr. Evans would let me go rather than risk the police or anyone getting involved. Seemed obvious that Jeri's MS had made me a weak link. I *never* intended for the plan to come off, Holt."

"No? Tell me, Riley, because that part's not making sense right now."

"The guy told me wrong about the timing of the bomb. It was supposed to go off before the catamaran even left the bay, and I rigged the engine to the same timer, so the fire would start just before the bomb. I knew it couldn't look like I'd messed up on purpose, or this guy'd never get off my back. It had to be a close call.''

"Yeah, it was that, all right!"

"I figured they'd get off the boat in time, and have an easy swim to shore, or some other boat would pick them up in the bay. When I found out Seth and Emma had been out at sea by the time the fire started and almost didn't make it…" He swallowed and shook his head, pressed the back of his hand across his eyes.

"But that hasn't stopped you from trying it again."

"He came back. Just last night. Same threats. Vague, you know? If someone *happened* to break in and rough her up. And Jeri's even worse now than she was a couple of months ago. She's not going to hang on much longer. Little Hayley's only seven years old. Jeri doesn't want to let go of life, doesn't want to leave the kids one minute before she has to, and when he talked about 'roughing her up' I just… Something that'd only make a bruise on a healthy person could be enough to kill her.''

"So you said yes."

"Just to get him to stop talking about someone hurting my wife. I have the gear in my bag, but I couldn't set it up. I couldn't do it. I guess I never intended to. I was just buying time, going through the motions, waiting for a miracle. It's all still here. You can see it, Holt. You can take it and show it to the police, or whoever. Whatever you want me to do, I'll do it."

"I need to think," Holt said. "I need to work this out."

Marisol watched him, wanting to say or do something that would help, but Holt seemed barely aware that she was still here. He leaned his forehead on the carbon fiber mast, with his forearm resting above it, and closed his eyes, shutting out the world.

She would have stepped close and massaged his shoulders, only she knew he'd push her away. She felt unnecessary and shut out. Just the messenger, to be thanked and sent away, kept in the dark. If she'd answered his apology differently this afternoon, would he be treating her differently now?

Probably not.

This was a part of his life that she wasn't involved in, and it underlined how tenuous their connection had been even at its best, on Tuesday night. How could he have said it was the best night of his life? It had meant nothing.

After a minute, Holt straightened again.

"Okay, here's the deal. Riley, you're coming with me and we're going to see Seth and Gideon and Marcus. I doubt they'll buy your story unless they hear it in person. I wouldn't have. And they'll have questions. They'll want any detail you can give them that might help identify the man who approached you."

"There's not much of that," Riley said. "He met me at night. Just came at me out of the shadows, after I'd stayed late at the boatyard. I got the impression he'd done stuff to change his appearance. The only thing I remember is that he had a cough."

"A cough?" Holt repeated. "Marisol, you heard that, too."

"Yes, I did."

"Like this, kind of." Riley imitated the sound with a series of high-pitched barks and gasps.

"That's close," Marisol agreed.

Holt checked his watch. "It's getting late. Marisol, I need to get you home so you can rest for tomorrow."

"What about your rest?" she answered.

"I'll grab what I can. This is more important." He grinned suddenly and cupped his hand around her jaw in a casual caress that she hated, even while it sent an electric pulse straight to her core. "Don't question it. It gives you an edge, so take it."

"I don't need an edge, Holt." She tilted her head, shying away from his touch. She didn't want him to see how even such a simple touch still affected her. "My boat can beat yours without one."

The evening with the navy officials had begun to break up by the time Holt had dropped Marisol at her father's house and arrived home with Riley Walker in tow. His anger against the other man had ebbed in the face of Walker's emotional words. A stronger man would have acted differently, but Riley had never been strong in that way.

He was a deeply devoted husband and father. Tonight's sorry tale had proved it. And he'd been a hardworking employee, content to stay in a position where he could take orders and avoid responsibility. He'd dealt with his wife's incurable degenerative illness in the same way he dealt with everything—plenty of love, not a lot of initiative, or planning for the future, too much quiet self-sufficiency.

Seth, Gideon and Marcus—who'd arrived from Virginia today—were grouped with four navy officials in the ocean room, finishing glasses of vintage port. Seth was the first one to turn and see Holt, who'd entered quietly after leaving Riley waiting in another room. With a questioning look, Seth strode over at once.

"Problem with *Unicorn?*"

"Kind of. Other kinds of creatures involved, too. Like flat, flappy, fishy things that live in the sea."

Seth swore. "Stingray," he muttered.

"So can you wind this up pretty soon?" Holt said. "There's someone I've brought that you need to talk to, and then we've got things to work out."

"It's winding up on its own. You want Gideon and Marcus to stay, right?"

"Definitely. Did the whole party show up tonight? All the officials that are taking tomorrow's tour?"

"No, there was a second group of three who arrived on a later schedule and went directly to their hotel."

Holt accepted a small glass of port and went to get introduced to the clutch of uniforms, knowing he'd suffer through the minutes of conversation that remained.

He kept thinking of Marisol.

Not where his focus should be.

Not where it would have been a week ago. On a woman? When he had to win a big race tomorrow? After detouring from his schedule in order to save the free world the night before?

Okay, saving the free world was a slight exaggeration, but this was important. Critically important. Front-page headlines important, only it was probably too top secret ever to reach the press. That kind of important. His brain kept telling him so, while his heart went right on aching, and his thoughts went right on circling over his past mistakes with Marisol and his potential future actions, like a radar signal circling around on a screen.

One of the naval officers looked at his watch and put down his glass.

"The car should be here," he said.

Holt looked at the stripes on his cuffs, at the colors arranged across his left breast, and at the way the other three officers put down their glasses, also, within seconds of his announcement. Easy to tell who was the boss.

Seth, Marcus and Gideon ushered the group out to their waiting vehicle and returned at once to Holt, who'd positioned himself at the closed door of the room in which Riley was waiting so there was no chance the other man would appear at the wrong moment.

"Who've you got in here, Holt?" Marcus asked in an undertone, looking at the solid wood of the door as if he was planning to acquire X-ray vision sometime within the next few seconds, to add to his existing arsenal of superhuman qualities. "You didn't seem to want our uniform guys to get a look at him."

"Not when one of them could well be the man who paid him to plant the bomb on Seth's catamaran three months ago," Holt said.

"We have to act as if everything is proceeding according to plan, or our guy will know something's up," Seth argued twenty minutes later.

He, Gideon and Marcus had listened to Riley's story, and Holt had called a cab to take the now-exhausted man home to his family.

"Our guy's going to be here somewhere tomorrow,

waiting for his chance, waiting for the distraction, and in contact with the other people who are working with him,'' Seth went on. ''He doesn't know Riley hasn't come through this time.''

''That's in our favor,'' Marcus said.

''The question is, do I go ahead and show the plans and the prototype?''

''We have to,'' Gideon argued. ''For the same reason that you just gave. If we don't, our probably asthmatic double agent will know something's up.''

''Only we could be showing the prototype to the Rebelian agent himself,'' said Seth.

''We've been told that was a possibility for a while.''

''Are you sure he's one of your visiting uniforms?'' Holt asked.

''Not sure,'' Marcus answered. ''But let's not rule it out. Let's keep it in view.''

''How much information could he get just from looking at the prototype?''

Suddenly, Holt felt out of the loop on this. Not the same way as his sister Laura had been a couple of months ago when Seth and their father had deliberately tried to keep her in the dark about the possibility of danger and sabotage in a misguided act of protection. Out of the loop just as effectively, however.

He'd focused so much on his racing, on building the Evans name by showcasing their winning boats, that he'd taken all this top-secret navy stuff for granted. Yeah, they were working on a project, and it was very exciting, and it mustn't be talked about, and Seth got a new worry line on his forehead almost every week because of it.

But he'd never seen the plans, never visited the high-security section of the huge Evans boatyard where the Stingray prototype was being built. It had a...what, a new propulsion mechanism, right? And an anti-sonar shield. And revolutionary silencing systems. And it was small and agile and fast.

But how? Why?

He didn't know any of that. Not his area. Not his concern.

Even during Seth's mock demonstration on the computer on Tuesday, Holt had played the role of a visiting naval officer with less than half his active brain. He'd taken in Seth's arguments at the time, found them convincing and let them slide from his memory immediately afterward, in favor of thinking about the winds, the currents and the race.

Suddenly, with his beloved *Unicorn* as a player in the game—the fall guy, for God's sake, the *decoy*—he wanted to come up with some input.

"He could learn a lot," Gideon said, in answer to Holt's question. "Problem is, we're getting two different channels of information from the Pentagon. On the one hand, the navy has told us to make the information available to these guys. Anything they ask for. Anything they want. They want us to sell them on this sub, and they believe the group they've sent is above suspicion."

"Okay, I get that," Holt said.

"On the other hand, a whole different section of the U.S. Defense Department is giving us intelligence that suggests there may be a spy. We shouldn't cancel the tour, we're told, but we should be aware, try to smoke him out if we can. Frankly, it's been frustrating, and Seth, you've had to spend more time than you wanted on trying to get these different departments to talk to each other so that they can present a consistent picture to us.''

"With not much of a result," Seth said. "I guess intelligence information turned up by one department isn't always acted on in the right way by another. Unfortunately, this time we're caught in the middle."

"Okay," Holt said again. He ground his fingertips into his temples. "Excuse me, I'm just getting my head around something here."

Wheels turned in his mind so fast he almost expected the others to hear a whirring sound. That word *decoy* he'd just used in his head…yacht racing…new designs…throwing the other competitors off the track…distracting them with a supposedly radical new keel design, when really it was the cut of the sails that gave you the edge.

Yes!

Or was it stupid, naive, impossible?

He'd soon find out.

"How about you make a few last-minute technical modifications to the prototype?" he said. "Gideon, that's not beyond you, is it?"

"Tell me what you're saying, Holt."

"You design, we'll program the computer and take some tools to the actual craft. Hack pieces off it."

"What?"

"Not really. Shave it a bit. Add some fins. You know what I mean."

"Starting to," Gideon said.

Marcus was grinning.

"Hack pieces off it? Add fins?" Seth clearly didn't know whether to laugh or cry.

"If it takes all night. Is that possible? This brilliant new Evans sub won't have the power or the stealth to cruise a bathtub by the time we've finished with her, and you've got the ability to make the changes so subtle, Gideon, that it wouldn't be obvious until they took away any stolen plans and figures and had a closer look."

"Yes." Gideon's otherworldly blue eyes—eyes that still sometimes acted as windows to the dark past he'd suffered as the mind-controlled captive of some very evil people—began to shine with a powerful light. "Yes. Change a couple of crucial ratios. Reconfigure the settings. I see what you mean, Holt."

"Before the Rebelians have a chance to realize that the data they've stolen is fake, we'd better have caught this guy," Seth put in.

"We don't have a lot to go on," Holt answered. "A distinctive cough. What's that worth?"

"But we know he'll be here," Marcus said. "Emerald Cove is a finite universe."

"A very crowded finite universe right now," Holt replied.

Seth looked at his watch. "It's nearly midnight. So far, we've got this, or nothing."

"We've got this," Gideon said. "And I like it. Let's get to work."

Thirteen

"**Y**ou're lying, you traitor," Holt croaked. "I should break you into a thousand pieces."

His clock radio alarm didn't reply directly to the accusation or the threat. It just kept up with its raucous burring sound. Holt fumbled at it, thumped it, turned it upside down, opened one eye, managed to focus on the controls and finally got it to shut up.

It was not, could not possibly be, seven o'clock. It was not, could not possibly be, a bare three hours until the start gun for *Unicorn*'s big race.

He got a second eye open and gauged the level of the light outside. Slanting. Fresh. Yellow. The clock was right.

Maybe he shouldn't have gotten into bed at all, two and a quarter hours ago, when he'd finally arrived home from the boatyard after he, Seth, Marcus and Gideon, along with an urgently summoned skeleton crew of three of Evans Yachts's longest-serving and most trusted technicians, had made Gideon's subtle modifications to the prototype and the plans.

His adrenaline had still been pumping then. He could have kept going.

But instead he'd done the sensible thing. He'd showered, stripped to his boxers and lain down, and the adrenaline had disappeared away like bath water down a drain, giving him around two hours of deep sleep and a feeling that resembled a bad hangover as he tried to drag himself awake again.

No member of any other crew, even the most casual amateur on the slowest cruise boat would sail today on so little sleep.

Marisol would have gotten to bed at around eleven. Right now she might be pulling herself from the pool after a lazy pre-breakfast swim. Fernando's house-keeper would be filling her with nourishment and cal-ories, lovingly prepared and arranged on a pretty plate. She'd take a shower, slather her face and neck and shoulders with sunscreen....

"I've got to stop thinking about her," Holt decided. "I hope she's thinking about me. I hope she's *obsessing* about me."

The same way he was obsessing about her. The way he should be obsessing about the race.

The race.

He lurched out of bed and headed for the shower, taking one step at a time, doing what he had to do.

A circular saw screamed and died and screamed again inside one of Evans Yachts's big boat sheds, as Seth, Marcus and Gideon ushered the group of seven naval officers into the yard. In the open air, a man sprayed the sleek hull of a pleasure cruiser with its final finish. In the office, the phone rang. Attached to a loud exterior bell so that it could be heard even when the office was unattended, it overtook the sound of the saw, which had just been switched off.

Business as usual at Evans Yachts.

This was just the way Seth had wanted it, and he

relaxed a fraction, hoping his lack of sleep last night wasn't as obvious as it felt. He decided to buy some more time, just to get focused, to get a better handle on these guys in the daylight and in an environment where he felt totally at home.

There was tension in the air this morning, and he hadn't identified its source. His own nerves? Gideon's heightened level of brain activity? He was wired after last night, though he concealed it well. Or was some of the tension coming from the naval officials themselves?

Yeah, he thought so, but he wanted a chance to get a closer look at the dynamics of the group before they opened Shed Three.

Seth loved this place. Loved the smells of wood and fiberglass and Kevlar and canvas. Loved the activity and the noise, and the fact that there was always something to see, always a boat at a different stage of production. Only over the last few months did he regularly make the time to come out here. And he enjoyed every minute. At least half of these navy men had spent their whole lives around harbors and boats, and should feel the same way he did. Maybe he could use that.

"As you probably know," he announced to the visitors, "we have a growing reputation for our attention to detail in restoring classic yachts. The boat you can see in the boatshed just over here was built in Germany in the twenties and discovered last year in use as a houseboat on the Rhine River. She was a wreck. Since we have a little time, if anyone would care for a closer look, we can go in and see what she looks like now. We tracked down the original plans of a sister boat with almost exactly the same design, and this one's shaping up even better than we hoped.''

Seth got an arrowing look from Marcus and a tiny nod from Gideon. They understood what he was doing, and they were trying to gauge the dynamics of the group in this setting, also.

Vice-Admiral Harry Mundle gave a curt nod. ''Sure. Let's take a look.''

All the officers wore civilian clothes today, but this man still behaved like the high-ranking officer he was. He dictated the pace and the focus, and the more junior officers and aides automatically followed his cues, which might make it convenient for anyone who didn't want to stand out from the group.

Seth saw the way Marcus's gaze flicked back and forth, in search of any clue that one of these men might not be genuine.

''You just don't get craft of this caliber anymore,'' Captain Paul Delphus said to the vice-admiral. ''Do you, sir?''

''Oh, I wouldn't say that. Although, yes, she's beautiful.''

''Coming up real nice, Seth,'' said Rob Hewitt, the marine carpenter who'd been using the saw.

''Go ahead with what you're doing, Rob,'' Seth told him. ''Don't let us hold you up. We're on a tight deadline with this boat, aren't we?''

''Getting tighter every day,'' Rob answered. ''She's stubborn. She lets us know if she's not happy with what we're doing to her and makes us start over.''

A copy of the sister boat's plans was laid out on the table, and Vice-Admiral Mundle bent over them, with Captain Delphus close beside him.

"Impressive," the senior officer muttered.

"Today's vessels are about science, but a boat like this is a work of art," Paul Delphus said. "This has to be very similar to another German boat I saw once, which had supposedly played host to Adolf Hitler."

"The way every castle in England once played host to Henry the Eighth," Mundle said, in a cynical drawl. He looked impatient now, and ready for business. "Can we move to Shed Three?"

"Of course," Seth agreed, interested in the way the vice-admiral let his impatience show, and interested in the mix of expressions he saw on different faces. Some of the officials wanted to get to the sub right away. Others had more patience, or at any rate they pretended to. Whatever they really felt, however, five of the officers moved to exit through Shed One's huge open door. Mundle would have done so, too, only Captain Delphus held him back.

"Look, sir, at the name of the boatyard and the designer, here on the plans," Captain Delphus said. "This is a sister, or at worst a cousin, let's say, to the boat I'm talking about."

Rob began to sweep up the sawdust he'd made a few minutes earlier when shaping the vessel's new planks. He knew when to step back out of the limelight.

"That's Shed Three?" said an aide, pointing across the yard to the large, windowless building that housed the prototype of the sub.

"Yes," Seth answered.

The group began to move across the yard, with Gideon and Marcus in the lead, and Seth himself bringing up the rear. Behind him, he heard Delphus still enthusing about the classic yacht, apparently oblivious to his senior officer's ebbing patience. "History jumps out at you when you least expect it, doesn't it?" he said.

"Fascinating," Mundle agreed.

Then one of the two men coughed, making a high-pitched wheezy, whistling sound. Seth turned in time to see Captain Delphus pulling an asthma inhaler from his pocket.

"I must insist on accompanying the other officers on the tour of the Stingray sub, as arranged!" the naval captain said, some minutes later in one of the boatyard's small offices. A vein stood out on his temple, against a background of high color. He was angry and tense, and it showed, despite his best effort at presenting a calm facade.

"I'm sorry, Captain Delphus," Seth answered in a neutral, pleasant tone. "We have an administrative issue that's come up."

"What issue?" The man had begun to sweat, Seth saw. This was the guy they'd been after since Riley Walker had sabotaged the catamaran back in June. He was sure of it.

"Your security clearance," Seth explained. "It's a bureaucratic bungle, I'm sure, but we received a fax asking us to hold you aside until the matter was cleared up."

He was making all of this up as he went along, and enjoying it, to tell the truth. It was a positive pleasure to turn this man's skin wet with agitation, or even fear, after what he and his cohorts had put everyone through. Seth thought of how narrowly he and Emma

had escaped with their lives, and he remembered the
unprovoked, unexplained and unsolved attack on Alison Myers, now his cousin Drew's fiancée.

Meanwhile, a pair of top-level agents in defense
intelligence were on their way to the boatyard to interview and undoubtedly arrest the naval captain.
They should be there within minutes. They'd asked
Seth to stall Delphus without raising his suspicions
until they got there. They'd also picked up another
man, less than an hour ago, in possession of a sophisticated laptop he wasn't using to write poetry, and
surveillance equipment that no innocent citizen should
need in a place like Emerald Cove.

"The guy rolled over like a dog with an itchy
back," one of the agents had told Seth on the phone.
"His name's Arnold Reeve. He's Rebelian by birth,
and an American citizen through his father, but basi-
cally he'll take money or a deal from anyone who's
offering. We're going to check back through his prior
activities very carefully. He fingered Delphus right
away in exchange for leniency, and he gave us some
pretty solid leads on the other Rebelian operatives in
town, although he claims they're part of a different
cell, and he only knows them by code names. We'll
have this wrapped up in another couple of days."

"What about Delphus himself?" Seth had asked.
"Is he just in it for the money, too?"

"No, he's a fanatical Rebelian patriot, our guy
claims, and he's acted covertly in the interests of the
Rebelian military through his entire U.S. naval career.
Until DeBruzkya's coup, he wouldn't have been much
of a threat to U.S. interests, fortunately. He may be
harder to break, but we have proof of his activities,

so getting him to talk would just be the icing on the cake.''

Cake, Seth thought, remembering the conversation with the defense agent just a few minutes earlier. That'd be a nice gesture, now, wouldn't it?

Aloud he said, still superbly polite, ''Could I get you a coffee? Maybe a sandwich or some cake while you're waiting, Captain Delphus?''

''I'm fine,'' the other man answered.

He squeezed out a fake smile, and Seth hid a real one. A weight lifted from his shoulders like a jet rising from a runway, and he decided that if Holt and *Unicorn* could just win their race today, things would be pretty near perfect at Evans Yachts.

The air felt like soup today, as humid as a sodden sponge. Even Holt, who was used to it, found it oppressive. Could be the lack of sleep. Could be another reason.

He wondered what was happening at the boatyard. The navy officials must be taking their tour right now. Seth, Marcus and Gideon must have their minds stretched like the rigging on a boat, singing with tensile strength. Sell the sub, finger the spy. When you had two goals, you had two ways to fail.

''Man, is it sticky today!'' said *Unicorn*'s helmsman, Greg Pearson.

''So it isn't just me?'' Holt answered.

''It isn't just you. How's that forecast?''

''Still not telling us enough of what we want to know. This race should be a walk in the park, but I have a feeling it's not going to be. Or maybe that's just signal interference from the rest of my life.''

"What's wrong with the rest of your life?" Greg asked.

Good one, Holt. You've just made the guy ask you a question you can't answer without blowing the lid on the two major things on your mental radar screen that you don't want to talk about. Marisol and the sub.

"It's going to hell in a hand basket, but that's all the detail I'm giving," he answered, glad this wasn't Mom he was talking to. "Gallon of coffee, and I should be fine. There's about a thousand members of my family expecting to see me in the Clipper Bar in three minutes, so can I stick you with taking care of this tub till I get back, Greg?"

The rest of the crew had begun to show up now, too.

"Sure," Greg answered. "I'll sit at the nav station and check the forecast a few more times, just for the heck of it."

"Sounds like a plan. See you in a bit."

The group of family and friends who had gathered in the Clipper Bar seemed as if they were there for a baby shower rather than a yacht race. Everyone cooed over Honey and Max's tiny Maxwell junior, and Gretchen and Kurt Miller's seven-month-old daughter, Violet. Marcus's wife Samantha had four-month-old Hank with her, and Seth's wife Emma stuck out her stomach and tried to convince everyone that her three-month pregnancy was showing, too. Emma had a dreamy expression on her face as she looked at the babies. Holt had seen this expression before.

He'd seen it, and he'd been terrified by it. Today he wasn't. Today he just kept wondering what the same expression would do to Marisol's face.

He'd bet she'd look more beautiful than ever.

And he not only wanted to *see* the expression, he wanted to be the man responsible for putting it there.

Okay, now *that* was terrifying.

Much more terrifying than yacht races, or secret navy contracts, or spies and plots and little European countries with megalomaniac leaders and nasty games to play.

"Any word on what's happening at the boatyard?" he asked his father quietly.

"Not yet."

"Can you believe this? That we're caught up in something like this? We're just a family with a business to run, for God's sake! Look at all these babies. Look at Gretchen, the sister Marcus never even knew about until a year ago. Ordinary mom and cryptology genius, all in the same package. I just want to race. I never wanted any of this."

"Then go race, Holt," his father said.

"Tell me what's happening. Any news, I want an update, even if I'm halfway to the Bahamas."

"Check your e-mail on the boat."

"Fax it to me, along with the latest forecast."

"The computer, the fax, the cell phone. Even during the race, you can still be a part of this. It's a metaphor, isn't it? Everything's connected, including Evans Yachts, and a country called Rebelia that we'd barely heard of this time last year."

"Help, Mom." Holt turned to his second parent. "Dad's getting deep and intellectual. Give him a beer before it gets out of control."

His mother came up and kissed him. "Win," she said. "Beat those storms. Use them."

"If they happen."

"And come back safe."

Even the sky concealed its intentions today. There were no obvious banks of cloud, but the atmosphere at the horizon looked slate-hued, rather than clear blue. The twenty-minute gun sounded and the bay was like a schoolyard thirty seconds before the bell—swarming, chaotic, noisy. *Unicorn*'s deck teemed with sailors, elbow to elbow, muscular and loud. Greg Pearson had the helm and jockeyed for the best start position.

"Tacking!" Holt yelled, and the coffee grinders ticked furiously as the mainsail swung across. The rigging sang and creaked.

At this critical moment, his cell phone vibrated against his hip and he grabbed it. After this one, he wouldn't be taking any more calls. He'd fling the thing below deck and not think of it again until he called home to announce—he hoped—victory. "Yup?"

"It's Seth," his brother said. "We got our Rebelian agent."

"That's great, Seth!"

"He's been taken for questioning, and they've arrested his accomplice, too, with good leads on the other cell still on the loose."

"Then this is over? It's all over." He could think about the race. He could think about Marisol, the best night of his life and the rest of his life, work out what it all meant without world events intruding, mocking him for his priorities. Holt felt a sweet wash of relief.

Naive relief.

Seth's silence told him so, almost at once.

"What's up, Seth?"

"Don't know. Might never know. But Marcus made a phone call a few minutes ago, and now he's got this look on his face. He's been involved in some pretty high-level covert operations in his time. If the U.S. sends in a team to overthrow DeBruzkya's dictatorship in Rebelia, I won't be surprised if it turns out he's a part of it."

"But he's got a baby to look after."

"I think that explains the look. I'm not saying anything to him. He obviously can't talk about it. Your part in this is over, Holt. Mine, I hope, will be limited to negotiating on the sub. The genuine navy officials were very happy with what they saw. But the rest of it may play out for a long time."

Holt swore.

"Win, okay?" Seth said. "That's your job. It's your only job today."

"Aye aye, Cap'n," Holt answered, and hoped he'd convinced Seth that he actually cared.

It came back when the start gun sounded.

The drive, the need, the fire in his belly—all of it came back.

Unicorn was third across the line, just seconds behind the lead boat, *British Blue. Omega* came in second, with the other two major maxi contenders, *Skyrider* and *Lavazzi* bow to bow a little farther back.

Holt saw Marisol climbing around on deck, yelling instructions, working the boat. Even at this distance, he didn't have the slightest trouble picking her out from the rest of the all-male crew. To the depth of his bones, he knew the way she moved, knew the shape

of her silhouette, knew how her black hair looked
when it was knotted on top of her head.

When they got to Nassau, he was going to push
harder. It can't end like this, he thought. I want to be
on the same boat, not fighting her.

The wind was good, steady and strong, and all the
boats had their spinnakers up, making a display of
lavish color that filled the bay. They left the shore
behind in minutes, and the slower yachts, competing
with each other rather than taking on the impossible
task of beating the maxis across the finish, soon
dropped from sight, as well.

Greg took the waves like a surfer, making his task
look simple and fun. Holt knew it was anything but.
A helmsman needed tireless stamina and strength, un-
broken concentration and an intuitive sense of wind
and current and waves. Yep, all of that, and yet still
Holt almost ached for his own turn at the wheel.

A couple of hours into the race, he went below to
the stripped-out racing interior, and gulped down a
meal before relieving his chief helmsman and rotating
the rest of the crew. The wind had picked up, he
found, and it was clocking around a bit now. The
slate-blue color in the sky had gotten darker and
moved closer. Those storms were no longer a theo-
retical possibility in the forecast; they were happening.
Would they help the winning boat to finish in record
time, or force half the fleet to retire?

Greg had had the easy stint at the wheel. These next
few hours would be a lot harder. Ahead, Holt saw the
first flash of lightning, and wondered why he'd ever
thought the sky was blue today.

Gray. That was gray up ahead, shading to black.

"This is okay," Greg said, watching the sky and the wind, also. "Might have to take down the spinnaker. Push through the weather, get out the other side, get to Nassau first."

They were lying in first place at the moment, with *Skyrider* and *Omega* both in sight off the starboard stern.

The wind died for a few seconds then shifted ninety degrees and came at them harder than ever. "Feel that?" Holt yelled above the rising volume of wind. The rigging protested and he had to wrestle with the wheel. The surface of the water had grown choppy, with white lacy bits that meant trouble. "It's going to get worse and it's coming on fast. Let's not wait. Get the spinnaker down now."

The crew worked like a machine and pulled the big sail in, stowing it below deck. Inevitably, *Unicorn* slackened speed, but she was less vulnerable to the changing winds this way, and easier to steer through the rapidly building waves.

"*Omega*'s bringing down their spin," Greg said, watching the other boat behind them. "Having trouble." He whistled and swore. "Nearly lost it over the side. Okay, no, they've got it in now."

"*Skyrider?*"

"Still flying. Powering in our direction. Cutting it real fine out there."

The wind clocked again, seventy, maybe eighty degrees back to its original direction. Didn't seem to like it there. Shifted yet again. Holt thought about the currents at this point, thought about water depth and wind speeds. "We're going to get some nice waves up ahead," he said.

A sailor's understatement. For *nice* substitute *evil*.

He pulled on the wheel. His arms would be dropping off after a couple of hours of this. He heard a ripping sound followed by urgent shouting, and was stunned to see *Skyrider* right off *Unicorn*'s starboard bow. Hell, he'd had no idea they were so close! He'd been staring at the waves and the wind, not even thinking about the other boats. *Skyrider*'s spinnaker had ripped into several huge pieces and now threatened to foul the rigging.

Crew swarmed frantically in the bows of the boat, hauling it in, yelling to each other. Marisol was in the thick of the action, yelling too. That was the second expensive sail that *Skyrider* had ripped in a week, and Holt wondered about the crew's dynamics on board. They should have pulled the big sail in ten minutes ago, or sooner. Who'd taken the decision on that one?

Still, he couldn't deny it—the other maxi had powered into the lead.

"It doesn't matter," Marisol said through clenched teeth, knowing that once again Holt had seen what happened.

She didn't care about the shredded sail in the same way she'd cared about the one they'd ruined during Monday's practice. Instead, she got an image flashing through her head of herself and Holt sitting in some waterfront bar in Nassau, several hours from now, while she talked through the mishap and got it out of her system.

It wouldn't happen. She wouldn't let it happen.

The best night of his life? Who was he kidding? How naive did he think she was?

"We got the sail in," she said to Renaldo. "We didn't foul the gear. It's not like we're going to need a spinnaker again today. And we should reef the main."

"Not yet," Renaldo said.

"You just stalled on the spinnaker until we lost it."

"And now we're in the lead."

"You're going to do what I say. Conditions are getting worse every minute. We're reefing the main."

Renaldo called out to the crew and they sprang into action, reefing in the mainsail to give it less surface area for the wind to hit. Twenty minutes and another two reefs later, Marisol wondered why they'd bothered.

"We're taking it down," she said. "And putting up the storm jib. This weather's not playing around anymore, and we're not going to, either."

Renaldo didn't argue. Didn't even give her a dark look.

The sky had lowered until it was just over their heads and Marisol almost felt she could have touched it. Visibility around the boat dropped to fifty yards, except when the lightning flashed. Someone emptied a brimming bucket the size of a mountain over their heads, and raindrops the size of huge tadpoles hit their faces. The wind whipped spray from the water's rough surface, so that the only way she knew what was spray and what was rain was by the taste of it on her lips and the sting of it in her eyes.

The heavens had darkened like day's end, although it could only be mid-afternoon. They wouldn't be breaking any course records on this race. It would be a late finish, if they finished at all, and there'd be boats limping into Nassau or Nicolls Town well into the night, and motoring back into Emerald Cove or even to Bimini and Miami if they got pushed far enough off course.

Marisol's sense of time got hazy. How long had they been racing? How long had they been inside this? It was way worse than the worst-case scenarios she'd interpreted from the weather data.

Some of the crew looked scared, and everyone was soaked to the skin, despite the weather gear they'd scrambled into just as the storm first hit. The driving rain and wind pushed water up sleeves, down necks, through waistbands. Although air and water temperatures were still warm, the wind added a chill factor that had left Marisol's lips numb and her ears frozen.

Visibility went way down, and the waves got higher. Renaldo had taken the helm after they'd raised the storm jib, and they'd narrowly avoided two rogue waves, thanks to his skill.

When the boat broached and almost rolled, it was no one's fault. One moment they were heeling to starboard, heading to the crest of a wave that threatened to break, and the next they'd righted and heeled hard in the opposite direction. The wind screamed at them. The mast and sail hit the water, the rigging protested like a living creature, and the crew below deck were flung violently against the side of the cabin.

Harnessed to the rail, Marisol dangled and clung, with her stomach in her mouth, until another wave helped the boat right itself again. Renaldo still wrestled with the wheel, white-knuckled and tangled in his harness. His hand and his face were both cut and bleeding, she saw. If he felt pain, or if he'd seen the blood, he gave no sign.

"Good work," she told him.

"I don't like this."

"You want to pull out of the race?"

"No."

"Neither do I." They were almost at the halfway point between Emerald Cove and Andros Island, their first possible landfall, and though the wind was erratic, it still came largely from behind. This wasn't a Formula 500 event where you could pull over to the pit and get out of the race. They had to keep sailing—to survive, if not to win.

Another rogue wave swamped the boat within two minutes, making the bilge pumps work to maximum capacity. The water streamed back off the deck when the wave ebbed, and Marisol automatically took mental inventory of their gear. Had everything held? Had anything ripped and gone over the side? No, it all looked okay, to a cursory examination.

Several of the crew had gotten ill and lay below deck, rigid and useless and green-faced. Not that they were needed right now. There was no place in this weather for the perfectly executed and coordinated maneuvers they'd worked on.

The last of the water drained away, and Marisol only saw the stress fracture at the base of the mast by pure chance. At first she thought her eyes were playing tricks, but no, it was real. Death to their hopes of a victory. Dangerous to their lives. And most definitely real.

"Renaldo," she yelled. "Look at that."

"What? Where?"

"The mast is cracked at the base. It must have happened when we almost rolled."

The handful of crew on deck looked in their direction and grasped at once that something was wrong. Xavier Gonzalez began to pick his way along the rail, fighting the wind and rain.

"We need to get the storm jib down," Renaldo shouted.

"Bare poles? Can you control her that way?"

"That mast is going to—"

He never finished. Neither of them saw the wave, and Xavier's warning shout made no sense to them. They were both still too absorbed in digesting the implications and the reality of a stress fracture in the most critical part of the rig. The wave, meanwhile, roared up from behind them and broke over the boat. The mast screamed as it sheared. Its stays tore and whipped around.

Instinctively lifting her arm to protect her face, Marisol felt a flick like burning flame across her wrist and knew that one of the stays had connected, cut deep and drawn blood. She forgot about it almost at once. Huddling with Renaldo beside the wheel, she heard rather than saw what happened as the wind lifted the newly freed mast and rammed it into the side of the hull like a spear, shattering the carefully crafted layers of foam and laminate and holing the boat.

Again, the wind tore at the mast, the one remaining sail, the rigging and the hull. Another wave came over them, and this time *Skyrider* rolled. Marisol felt the water close round her and over her head before she had time to understand what had happened. Time slowed, and a ghostly green light filtered through the

water. She held her breath, but the lungful of air would
run out soon. Like the other crew who'd been on deck,
she was tethered to the boat, and she saw them working frantically to release their harnesses so that they
could swim to the surface for air.

Don't panic, she coached herself. Just get the harness free. Her right hand hurt when she tried to use
it, and it was bleeding, so she worked with her left.
Held her breath. Didn't panic.

Before she could free herself, the boat righted itself
to a sideways position, and she gasped precious air.
The rest of the crew were doing the same, and no one
on deck looked seriously hurt. Meanwhile, the tangled
mess of broken mast, torn rigging and sodden sail
floated like some bizarre form of jellyfish in the turbulent water, keeping the hull on its side. *Skyrider*
wouldn't stay afloat for long.

The crew who'd been below deck struggled to leave
the cabin. Jose Aguilera and Mike Tucker dragged one
of the self-inflating life rafts from the hold, yelling at
other crew members to do the same. There were four
rafts altogether, each of them able to hold six people.
The first raft inflated too soon, making conditions on
the near-vertical deck even more difficult to handle.

They tethered the raft to the boat and someone
yelled out the old sailors' wisdom, "Wait until you
have to step up to it, before you get in."

The line usually got a laugh, but it didn't today.
When the boat started to go down, they would indeed
be stepping up into the raft. It was the very last resort.

Marisol managed to reach the cabin, and found that
Swedish navigator Axel Svensson had wedged himself
into the nav station and was already on the radio, giv-

ing a Mayday call. It was answered at once, and Axel
reported, calm and clear, "We are getting the life rafts
on deck. We are dismasted, holed and laying down.
Repeat, this is *Skyrider* and we are dismasted and
holed. Our rig is in the water."

"I'm getting out the E.P.I.R.B. and the flares," she
told him. "The boat's going down, and when the rafts
start to drift we want at least one of them carrying a
signal. No injuries down here?"

"No, we're fine, I think."

They both looked around the sodden, cluttered
cabin, and only then did they see Bjarne, unconscious
and flung out on the ruined spinnaker like a rag doll,
his hand still bandaged from his accident during practice six days ago.

"Dios mio," Marisol whispered.

The radio crackled again, and she and Axel both
heard a new voice on the airwaves. *"Skyrider,* this is
Unicorn. We've seen your situation, and we're standing by to assist you."

Fourteen

Holt had seen the whole drama unfold aboard *Sky-rider,* and knew it was luck more than anything else keeping *Unicorn* still in one piece. He sensed that the storm center had almost passed over them. There hadn't been any lightning for a while. The rain still flooded down, but the wind had begun to ease, which meant that the seas would soon do the same.

For the moment, however, the waves were still enormous, unpredictable and threatening to break over his deck. Greg had taken the helm again, fighting the sea every inch of the way, and they quickly closed the distance between *Unicorn* and *Skyrider.*

Below deck, radio traffic made it clear that several other boats were also in trouble, particularly some of the smaller craft at the rear of the racing fleet. Closer to their own position, *Lavazzi* had a delaminating hull and was taking on water.

With no electrical storm on shore, and the storm moving to the northeast, at least two rescue helicopters had already left their bases, headed this way, and more had been summoned from farther afield. There were three commercial vessels also in the area, standing by to take on crew from the stricken yachts. For many boats, the outcome of the race had already become immaterial.

Not knowing how much longer *Unicorn*'s radio would remain operable, Holt yelled out his plan in short phrases, and waited for agreement from the other boat. He heard a crackle and the start of a word, and then nothing. *Skyrider*'s radio and electrical systems must have just failed. Lord, they didn't have much time, in that case, and they had twenty-two sailors to get across.

"We're going to need one of the choppers," he told Greg. "If we can't get them all on board before that boat goes down and they take to the rafts... We'll radio for assistance from one of the commercial boats, also. Off-load *Skyrider*'s crew to a bigger boat as soon as one gets here. And there may be crew with injuries."

The next half hour was a chaotic mess of action and effort and confusion in which the order of events blurred in Holt's mind even as they happened. *Unicorn*'s crew began to winch men across from *Skyrider,* one by one, while those who were left on board kept frantically working to keep the crippled vessel afloat. *Unicorn* got a radio report that a commercial fishing boat was headed this way.

His voice heavy with fatigue, Xavier Gonzalez reported as soon as he reached *Unicorn,* "We have a man unconscious below deck."

"We've radioed for a rescue chopper," Holt told him.

What if the boat didn't stay afloat until it got here? Lord, what was happening over there?

Holt saw Marisol and two others tether themselves to the rail. They managed to cut away the torn remnants of *Skyrider*'s rigging. When the last of it ripped away, the hull righted itself once more and the crew began to bail by hand. Their engine had died, of course, rendering their bilge pumps inoperable. Incredibly, they bailed effectively enough to make the boat lighten a little in the water, and for about five minutes Holt actually thought they might save her. If the fishing boat got here in time, and they could rig up a towline...

He heard a chopper in the distance and fought his way below deck to give the chopper crew a status report via the radio. Unconscious man. Three *Skyrider* crew still on board. Vessel afloat for the moment.

The chopper positioned itself overhead in a dangerous hover, with wind and waves fighting its attempt to stay level and still. Holt didn't have time to watch. The next crew member was on the wire, crossing the lethal stretch of turbulent water between *Skyrider* and *Unicorn,* and if the boats got washed apart and the line snapped...

"They're winching someone down to pick up the one who's unconscious," he heard one of his own crew report.

"They've got him on deck. Rescue medic has him in a sling. They're going up together."

"Next guy's on the wire here."

"Who's left?"

"Just their captain."

Marisol.

"Wave!" someone yelled.

"Big wave! Watch out!"

It hit while Renaldo Tejerizo was halfway across. The line went slack, then whipped taut and it was a miracle that it didn't break. Renaldo disappeared beneath the water then jerked into the air.

The wave had hit *Skyrider*, too, swamping her low-lying deck. The yacht wallowed like a dying whale. It rolled in the water, getting lower and lower, and Holt realized with a cold shock that Marisol was still tethered to the rail.

Hell, what was she doing? The boat was going down. The single inflated life raft snapped its line and went flying off across the water like a kite. Marisol wasn't in it.

"She can't get her harness unclipped," someone said.

"Is she hurt?"

"Looks that way. She's doing it one-handed. Left-handed."

Overhead, the rescue medic and his patient were still rising into the chopper. By the time the medic got the man unharnessed and was ready to descend again, it would be too late.

"Give me the line," Holt said. "I'm going in."

Too late to use the winch. He'd have to swim. The rogue wave had washed the two boats close together—the only thing in his favor. Marisol had slid off the deck and into the water, still battling desperately to free herself from the line.

Holt hit the water seconds later. I've had this nightmare before, he thought. Most people had them at some point in their lives. Endless film footage playing in the brain as you ran from mortal danger, but made no ground, or swam with bursting lungs and only got dragged farther and farther back by an unseen, implacable current.

This wasn't a nightmare, though. It was real. He had to get to Marisol before her boat went down. He made headway, could see the white shape of the hull looming in his vision, level with his own body and scarcely more visible in the water than he must be. He was only a few yards from Marisol now and could see her struggle to free herself getting more frantic and less effective at the same time. What was wrong? Had she gotten hurt? She wasn't using her right hand at all.

And then, in the space of two strokes of his arms, Marisol and the boat had vanished. Dear God, they'd just gone.

Holt dove beneath the gray, opaque surface of the water into a sudden eerie, resonant silence, found her just ahead of him and seized her body blindly, already fighting for breath. He didn't have time to see if she was conscious, in control, holding her breath, aware, *anything*.

His whole focus was on that harness, that single metal clip that he had to find and unfasten within the next few seconds or the boat would pull them both down beyond reach of the surface, down where there was no chance of either of them getting another breath ever again. It never entered his head that he could abandon her, that he wasn't tied to the drowning boat the way she was. He'd never let the boat take her to her death alone.

Here! This was it. He had it in his hands. The sheer intensity of his desperation made his fingers work and he saw, in increasing darkness, the blessed sight of the line and the clip separating, moving apart. He didn't realize how far the boat had already dragged them down until Marisol was freed. Kicking frantically, pulling on her arms, he urged her to swim, but for one horrifying moment, he lost his sense of which way to go.

Up? Where was up in all this weight of water and darkness?

With his last glimpse of the white mass of *Sky-rider*'s hull disappearing into the depths, the universe righted itself again. That was down. This was up. He felt Marisol begin to kick, also, and hauled her with him toward the holy light of the surface, far too distant. By the time they broke the water, half a lifetime later, his lungs were burning, yelling, treacherously close to sucking in seawater, and he dragged in air with a flood of relief so intense that every other muscle in his body let go.

"I love you," he said, holding on to her sweet, sweet body for dear life. "We're alive and I love you, Marisol."

In his arms, Marisol didn't answer. She just shuddered and panted and sobbed. Maybe she was shaking her head. Hell, would she really do that? Now? After what they'd just been through, and what he'd just said? Holt saw a black shape in the corner of his vision and heard a splash.

"She's hurt?" yelled the rescue paramedic. "I'll take her up first. You're okay to wait?"

"I'm fine," Holt said.

"That was a close call," the paramedic said.

"A taste of hell." Despite the seawater and rain that he swallowed every time he breathed, this was still heaven by comparison, purely because he had air.

"You still have a line to the other boat?" the paramedic shouted.

Do I? Holt wondered vaguely. "Uh…"

"You do. Don't detach it yet. Make sure it's not tangled around you, or around us when I take her up." The rescue paramedic secured Marisol and himself in the sling and rose from the water. Another wave rolled in, dunking them again before they could get clear, and water poured from their bodies as they went up.

Holt waited in the water, wondering why it seemed to want to drag him down. Sea boots, he realized. He still had his sea boots on. With an incredible effort, he kicked them free and shed his useless wet-weather gear, also.

As he unzipped the jacket, he noticed that he'd cut three of his fingers. Deep. Clean. The slits in his skin parted in the water like fish gills. He had no idea when it had happened. He tried to feel pain there, but couldn't. Looking up again, he saw a gray, squarish shape against the moving horizon and realized it was the fishing vessel they'd summoned by radio. How come he could see it so clearly?

Then he realized that was blue sky over there. The storm was passing.

The crew would survive this. *Unicorn* would survive this. Holt's boat had sustained minimal damage. He'd get on the helicopter radio and tell them to keep going. Greg would skipper the boat. It would reach the race finish in Nassau tonight. It might get its mainsail and spinnaker up again. It would probably even win. Holt wouldn't be on board, however. He'd be with Marisol.

"Ready?" Here was the human tea bag again, slick and black in his wet suit.

"Very!" Holt answered.

"Detach your line. We don't want to tie any knots, here."

"Yep. Sure." Except that he couldn't do it at first. His fingers kept saying they'd done enough for today. He lifted them from the water and saw an unholy amount of blood streaming from those deep slits in his skin. He hoped there weren't any sharks around.

"Here, I'll get it," the paramedic said.

"No, I'm doing it." Last effort. Last thing he had to do. Apart from talking to Marisol. Getting some kind of answer from her. He'd just told her he loved her, and she hadn't replied.

"I'm Tony, by the way."

"Holt. Good to meet you, Tony."

"I'm putting the sling around you now."

"That's great."

They rose from the jaws of the ocean, toward the hovering chopper overhead. On board, Tony unharnessed him, wrapped him up, tried to take a look at him and get him to lie down, but he wasn't having any of that. Not yet.

The unconscious crew member had begun to stir. Bjarne. Holt had met him a couple of times. The young Dane muttered as he came to the surface of awareness, and Holt knew this was a good sign. He'd be okay.

Marisol lay in a stretcher, blanketed tightly, her face white, her eyes open and calm, her right arm the only part of her body that showed. She looked…just beautiful. The most precious thing in the world. The woman for whom Holt would have gone to his death at the bottom of the sea. He almost fell to the floor of the chopper beside her, dimly aware that the second paramedic had prepared bandages and a splint for her injury. The helicopter rose out of its hover and sliced across the water.

"You didn't answer me back there," Holt yelled above the engine noise. "Yesterday, too. I told you Tuesday was the best night of my life. I told you I loved you. And it didn't get through."

"It got through," Marisol said, then spoke to the paramedic, her voice weak and vague. "What are you doing to my arm?"

"It didn't get through," Holt repeated. "You pushed me away. You didn't answer."

"I'm dressing and splinting it," the second paramedic said in answer to Marisol's question. "You've cracked your radius and ulna, and sliced the outside of your wrist through to the bone."

Marisol turned back to Holt. "Because I don't believe you," she said. "I just can't believe you." Then she craned her head up off the stretcher, looked down at her injured, bleeding arm and fainted.

"Okay, it's looking a lot prettier now. Can you hear me, Marisol?"

"Mmm," Marisol nodded. She was still in the helicopter.

"You've got a pretty bandage on your arm," the paramedic shouted. "No blood. Nothing gory to look at anymore. Want to open your eyes and talk to me?"

"Okay."

She saw the paramedic's face up close, frowning.

What was his name? Brian, she remembered. The other one, Tony, was talking to Bjarne, asking him where he was, what day it was, and who was the king of Denmark.

"Denmark has a king, right?" Tony asked.

"Queen. Queen Margrethe the Second."

"Great. You're doing great, Bjarne. I'm just going to check you out a little more, okay? We'll be getting you guys to the hospital soon."

Someone held Marisol's hand.

Holt.

Marisol felt a rush of warmth and relief and need that she still couldn't trust, still didn't feel safe about. She turned her head and looked at him. He sat in an awkward crouch, eyes closed, blanket around his shoulders, fingers of one hand roughly wrapped in gauze padding. He looked miserable, exhausted, hurt, lost. Her heart flipped painfully.

What had he said in the water? That he loved her? She tried not to want so desperately for it to be true.

He'd just saved her life. People said things like that, in acute circumstances.

"Thank you," she told him.

He looked up.

"For saving my life."

"Any time."

"You can get me to say it, you see. Any second, I'm going to say it."

"Say what, sweetheart?"

"What you want," she explained. "Even when I don't believe you, I still want to say it back. That I love you. That's self-destructive but I can't help it. I love you anyway. I just love you."

He sat up straighter, and some of the hurt and the misery drained away. That was good. Marisol vaguely understood that she never wanted Holt to look so stricken and so bereft of life and joy. "But you just told me…"

"That I don't believe you when you say it. I don't. Unfortunately for me, *you* can believe it when *I* say it. Because it's true. I've jumped on the bandwagon with all the others, Holt. I've fallen hard. Isn't that handy for you?"

"Is that what you think?"

Surprised, she realized that now he was angry.

"Is *that* what you think? Still?" he repeated, angrier than ever, and her hazy mind jolted back into focus. "How can you insult me like that?"

"Let's keep the patient calm," Brian said.

"No." Marisol shook her head with vigor. "I'm not good at calm. I'm not doing calm right now."

The cityscape of Miami slid into her vision. Freeways, apartment buildings, malls, playing fields, parking lots, a hospital with a helipad on its roof. She remembered how she'd seen an emergency helicopter landing here just a week ago, on her first visit to Diego.

She'd been so confused and uncertain about her feelings that day. She'd wanted answers, presented with the stark clarity and drama of a rescue chopper landing on a roof. She'd wanted to look at Diego in his hospital bed and know with no shadow of a doubt that she loved him.

It hadn't happened.

Not with Diego.

But it had happened with Holt.

"You're insulted?" she asked him. "You're angry?" She sat up, miles from calm, wanting Holt's emotions and hers right on the table. All of them. This minute. Before the chopper touched down.

"Damn straight," he said.

"Why?"

"Work it out," he growled.

"No. I want you to tell me. I want to know if I've worked it out right. I don't think I have." Her hair was cold and wet, glued together by the seawater into salty ropes. She brushed it back from her face with her one good hand and glared at the golden, perfect man who sat beside her.

He didn't look so golden and perfect right now. He had white patterns of salt crusted on his skin, dry lips, damp hair, a scowl across his face and anger-stiffened limbs. She loved him even more this way.

"I'm human, okay, Marisol?" he shouted. "I can feel things. Pain. My fingers are throbbing right now. And so's my heart. We've known each other, as adults, for a week. And this whole week I've gone with my gut on how I feel about you, and how you feel about me. The future we could have together, that we're meant to have together. I've pushed. I've said what's inside me. And you obviously think that I do that very casually. Every week. With every woman. But I don't."

"No?"

"I've only said it to you. Ever. And it hurts to have you dismiss it. Hurts to have you take your own feelings seriously, but not mine. I would have gone down with you and the boat today, before I stopped trying to get you freed. We both would have drowned. If you

can't trust my words, can you at least trust that? Think
back. Remember every second of it.''

"Oh, Holt.''

She closed her eyes, did as he'd urged and, yes, the
images came back. Her increasingly frantic struggle
to free herself from the line. Her treacherous lungs
bursting to take that final, fatal breath that would draw
in seawater not air. The boat already sinking to the
distant sea floor, dragging her with it.

And then Holt, there beside her, appearing like a
miracle, with fingers that worked faster than she could
see. It had taken them an agonizing length of time to
claw their way through the water and back to the surface. She'd slowed him down, and yet he hadn't left
her.

"You were a long way down, and I was still with
you, Marisol,'' he said. "I fought that harness and we
sank together. When we got to the surface, I told you
I loved you with my first breath. That's not about
delivering an easy line to get a woman into bed. That's
life and death. That's forever.''

"Forever? You want me forever?''

"I want you forever.'' He looked into her eyes, and
stroked scratchy, shaking fingers across her cheek.
"You have to believe me now, Marisol, because I
don't know what more proof there could be.''

Oh, dear God, yes!

"I believe you. I love you, Holt. Forever.'' She
burst into tears, and he wrapped his arms around her
as if he'd never let go.

"Let's please not kiss the patient right now,'' yelled
Brian. The helicopter lowered to the hospital rooftop,

sending downdrafts and engine noise billowing out on all sides.

"Yes, please let's kiss the patient," Marisol said to Holt, as the noise began to die away.

"Whatever the lady wants," he answered, and touched his mouth to hers.

"They're keeping me overnight for observation," Holt told his brother, several hours later, lying in his hospital bed. "At some point, I got some cuts—" He lifted his bandaged hand. "—and a bump on the head that I don't remember. I might be concussed, so if I start acting strangely…"

"You're already acting strangely," Seth answered. "You're marrying Marisol Villoria, and the two of you have only known each other for a week."

"A lot longer than that," Holt protested.

"Okay, correction, you've only *liked* each other for a week."

Liked? Seth thought he merely *liked* Marisol? She was on a different floor of the hospital, also under observation, and Holt already missed her like hell. He suppressed a groan. "I'd have thought you'd understand how I feel, Seth, after seeing the way you and Emma behave around each other."

Seth dropped his voice to a gruffer pitch. "I do understand. I just like teasing my playboy baby brother."

"Save your breath. I want to hear more details on the situation with the sub and the Rebelians. One spy cell is under arrest. The other's about to be. But that alone doesn't topple DeBruzkya's regime. Don't tell me it's going to play out through diplomatic channels and take years, when he's such a murdering despot, illegally in power, and the whole Rebelian nation lives in misery.''

"You've gotten beyond my level of security clearance with that one, Holt. Marcus says they have a lead on how to get him. As I said at the start of the race, I won't be surprised if he gets shipped out on a mission pretty soon.''

"A mission involving DeBruzkya?''

"We shouldn't talk about it. Tell me about your wedding plans.''

"Plans? Weddings have to be planned?'' Holt grinned. "Some of us have been unconscious today, we haven't had a chance to get all that far with making plans.''

And yet...

He already had some pretty firm ideas in place about how it would be. Soon, for a start. And in Spain, where the air would be filled with exotic scents and dazzling Mediterranean light. Crowded, because of all the people they'd want to invite. Noisy, because a lot of those people would be sailing types who knew how to party.

Thinking of Marisol, nothing but Marisol, Holt could hardly wait.

Epilogue

"It is good to know that my daughter is getting a man who deserves her," Fernando Villoria announced in English and then in Spanish to the wedding guests grouped around laden tables on the terrace at Marisol's grandmother's house in Ronda, Spain, two months later.

The line drew two successive waves of laughter.

"*Exactamente!*" Marisol agreed. The word needed no translation. Holt grinned at her, and she blushed. He took her hand in secret, in a nest of bridal tulle and silk beneath the cloth-draped table.

"And a man whom she deserves," Papa continued in English. "I have always wanted my daughter to deserve the things she obtains in life. It has been hard on her. I will be the first to admit that. If she had been of a different personality, I might not have treated her this way. But just as a high-quality metal must be tempered in a furnace to achieve its greatest strength—" He stopped, and turned to Marisol. "Happiness. That's all I've ever wanted for you, my beloved daughter." He raised his glass. "*Felicidad.* Happiness. To my daughter and her groom."

Glasses clinked together. Guests drank and applauded. Marisol's grandmother dabbed tears from her eyes. Evans women did the same, while Evans men cleared their throats and acted as if the collars on their shirts were suddenly too tight. Drew Evans kissed his new wife Alison and they exchanged a private smile, then Drew lifted his stepson Kevin high in his arms so that Kevin could see. Laura Evans's fiancé, Austin, passed her a clean handkerchief from his pocket. Villoria brothers hugged and clapped each other on the shoulder, while Villoria wives indulged their children with whatever they wanted to eat and drink. Sailors almost unrecognizable in their formal clothing joshed each other and looked for more beer. The terrace seemed crowded with children and babies, from all sides of the Evans and Villoria clans. It hadn't yet been established whether the children of the Extraordinary Five—now six—would inherit any of their parents' special abilities, but by anyone's standards they were bright, adorable, gifted babies.

Gretchen and Kurt's little Violet was cruising around the furniture, nearly ready to walk, and Gretchen had to spend most of her time holding the back of Violet's dress to keep her safe. Samantha's six-month-old Hank had just learned to crawl and wanted to practice across the tabletop. Faith and Luke's son babbled as if he thought people could understand his every word.

The non-extraordinary babies were, well, pretty extraordinary, too, Marisol considered. Standing out with his fair coloring amongst her Villoria nieces and nephews, with their gorgeous dark eyes, Honey Evans Strong's little son, Max junior, was now two and a half months old, and smiling up a storm.

With four months to go until scheduled to give birth herself, Emma Carpenter Evans didn't seem to know which baby to coo over most, and Seth indulged her every step of the way. Connor Quinn and Jake Ingram, and their wives Alyssa and Mariah, looked as if they could hardly wait to discover for themselves what the fuss with pregnancy and babies was all about.

Sadly, not everyone could be present at this November wedding. Gideon and Brooke's baby was due within a few weeks, so they'd regretfully declined their wedding invitation. Meanwhile, Marcus had been absent from home for over a month, on his covert mission. For Samantha, it was a difficult time, and Marisol knew she must ache at the thought that Marcus was missing such a cute stage in their son's development. Samantha had apparently received a phone call from Marcus at her hotel in Marbella just last night.

"He thinks he'll be able to make it here before we're all due to fly home," she'd reported last night at a big family dinner. "He sounded good. Tired. Satisfied."

"Does that mean what I think it means?" Holt had asked his cousin's wife. "DeBruzkya is history?"

"I can't say. Marcus couldn't say. I switched on the TV news this morning, and the situation in Rebelia is chaotic, apparently. No one's seen DeBruzkya for several days. That has to be good news. That, and the sound of Marcus's voice on the phone." Samantha had gotten teary at that point, and they'd all had to content themselves with assuming the best. Today, with happiness brimming inside Marisol like a fountain, the best seemed like the only possible outcome.

Looking around the festively decorated terrace, she

saw a wedding guest whom she'd never expected this time last week.

Was it purely a coincidence that a certain Miami nurse named Caroline Meiklejohn had been taking a vacation in Spain right now? Since she spoke only a few words of Spanish, Diego Ruiz, who looked ten years younger than he had in the hospital two months ago, had appointed himself as her host and tour guide, and hadn't left her side all day.

They looked very much absorbed in each other at this moment. In fact, no one paid any attention to the bridal couple at all. Characteristically, Holt seized his opportunity.

"Let's please kiss the bride?" he whispered. "Right now?"

Marisol recognized the variation on a now-familiar line, first heard against the beat of chopper blades two months ago, and cherished for all the dramatic memories it brought.

"Lo que el senor quiere," Marisol answered, smiling at her new husband. He'd begun to learn Spanish, since they intended to divide their time between Marbella and Emerald Cove. So far, however, he hadn't made a lot of progress—they'd had other priorities to focus on—so she translated. "Whatever the gentleman wants."

SILHOUETTE Romance™

Escape to a place where a kiss is still a kiss...
Feel the breathless connection...
Fall in love as though it were
the very first time...
Experience the power of love!

Come to where favorite authors—such as
Diana Palmer, Stella Bagwell,
Marie Ferrarella and many more—
deliver heart-warming romance and genuine
emotion, time after time after time....

Silhouette Romance—
stories straight from the heart!

Silhouette®
Where love comes alive™

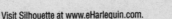

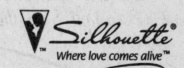

Where love comes alive™

From first love to forever, these love stories are
for today's woman with traditional values.

Silhouette® Desire

A highly passionate, emotionally powerful
and always provocative read.

SPECIAL EDITION™

Emotional, compelling stories that capture the
intensity of living, loving and creating a family in
today's world.

Silhouette®

INTIMATE MOMENTS™

A roller-coaster read that delivers romantic thrills
in a world of suspense, adventure and more.

Visit Silhouette at www.eHarlequin.com

SDIR2